Will's War in Brighton

By Nisse Visser

Will's War in Brighton
Nisse Visser
1st CBS/Ingram edition
May 2015 Amsterdam
ISBN/EAN: 978-90-823229-0-3
Netherlands NUR-CODE 337

3rd CBS/Kindle Edition
May 2015 Amsterdam
ISBN/EAN: 978-90-823229-1-0

a C.B.S. Green Man Publication
Cider Brandy Scribblers
Burnham-on-Sea, Somerset, England

Text copyright © 2014 **Nils Visser**
The Wyrde Woods Chronicles

Cover Illustration **Nick Bulters**
Interior illustration **Kayleih Kempers**

Registered at the *Depot van Nederlandse Publicaties*
Koninklijke Bibliotheek, Den Haag, The Netherlands

Instructions for use: Start at the beginning and read all the words
one after the other until you come to the very end and then stop.

Dedicated to Brightonians,
wherever they may be

I owe a special thanks to Bren Hall who proofread, edited, added suggestions, conducted research and encouraged me when I had doubts about my ability to portray a seaside town she is bonded to in a time period preceding my personal experience. Her support was a crucial ingredient.

I owe a great deal to the digital communities of Sussex-in-History, Brighton-Past, Marine Square & Kemp Town Brighton Past & Present and the 1940s World for their interest, input, feedback and support.

I am also very grateful to Nick Bulters and Kayleih Kempers for their interpretations of Will's War, I could not have got better work from them.

Table of Contents

1. THE CIRCUMNAVIGATION OF BIRMINGHAM

It was like being woken from a pleasant dream. Rudely so.

"Well young Maskall? Are you going to answer my question?" Mr. Hutchinson frowned at Will Maskall who just stared at him, feeling mute and helpless.

Only a moment before Will had been leaning over his desk; engrossed in the Spitfire fighter plane he had been drawing in his notebook and regretting that his twelve years made him far too young to join the RAF there and then. It looked like he would sit out the war in Brighton whilst others got to fight the Jerries. The Spitfire and associated thoughts had become his sole focal point so he had no idea what Mr. Hutchinson had been going on about in his monotonous nasal tone.

It wasn't that Will was an unwilling student but attending school meant listening to lectures all day long. There was nothing to do. Will liked to get his hands on things. Usually he managed to listen -for a while anyway- but Hutchinson never got to the point and traced ponderous side paths in his monologues which were hard to make sense of. The performance of a Spitfire's Rolls-Royce Merlin engine was far more interesting and of much greater relevance.

"Erm, Birmingham?" Will suggested rather lamely.

He vaguely recalled that Hutchinson had droned on about canals in the industrial Midlands last week and to say nothing would be worse as he knew from painful experience.

He made his eyes as wide as he could. Some adults were susceptible to this, claiming the clarity of his bright blue eyes and golden hair reminded them of an innocent angel. Will was anything but an angel and he knew his play-acting was in vain with Mr. Hutchinson.

"Birmingham." Mr. Hutchinson repeated, frowning. He was doing a little performance of his own now for the benefit of the other pupils in the classroom. "So you, William Maskall, claim that Captain James Cook was the first man to ever circumnavigate and map Birmingham in 1769?"

The other children laughed dutifully and Will grinned foolishly.

Then he took a deep breath, he knew Mr. Hutchinson well enough to know he would receive punishment anyway and it would be better to go down fighting like a proper hero.

"Indeed sir," he spoke loudly. "He sailed on them industrial canals you've been telling us about sir, on account of nobody else ever wanting to go to Birmingham but him."

A lot of boys sniggered and a few girls giggled but many of the children threw a cautious glance at their teacher as they did so. Mr. Hutchinson looked angry.

"To my desk if you please Maskall," the teacher said curtly and procured a wooden ruler from his top drawer.

Will stood up immediately; he dreaded the coming punishment but didn't want show this to the rest of the class. He wasn't some timid lass after all, he was almost a man. He'd be thirteen soon and then it would just be a year till he could quit this schooling and find himself a job, maybe even an apprenticeship so he could really learn something useful and master a trade. He sauntered to the front of the classroom as if he didn't have a care in the world.

"Both hands," Hutchinson glared. "Palms down."

Will laid both hands on the teacher's desk and gave an advance apology to his knuckles. He took a deep breath as Mr. Hutchinson raised his ruler but looked at the teacher defiantly. It had been a good jest, he reckoned.

Just then a distant sound wafted in through the open windows; a sound which Will had both come to dread and anticipate: The ominous wail of the air raid siren. Rising and then falling before repeating its eerie call again and again.

"Right boys and girls, you know what to do," Mr. Hutchinson said. "To the bomb-trenches this instant, don't forget your gas masks."

The children jumped up and all semblance of order was gone in an instant as some had to go back to their desks where they had left their gas masks despite the instructions not to do so. Will made to return to his desk to retrieve the metal tubular container which contained his gas mask.

"Wait just one moment, Maskall," Hutchinson snapped at Will. "Hands."

Will reluctantly laid his hands on the desk again and the teacher snapped his ruler against them once, then twice.

Will clenched his teeth as pain shot through his knuckles. Mr. Hutchinson was breaking the rules; there wasn't supposed to be a second's delay when the sirens sounded. Will was pretty sure Hutchinson would be in trouble if a Heinkel bomber made mincemeat out of Will just because he didn't get to the trenches in time.

"Very well, lad, fetch your gas mask."

3

Will rushed to his desk, his hands smarting. He was the last to depart the classroom where he joined the flow of pupils in the corridor. The air raid sirens had stopped at last but that meant nothing till the all-clear sounded.

2. AIR RAID WARNING

When they poured out of the school the children cast anxious looks at the blue sky, afraid of seeing the dreaded silhouettes of German bombers descending upon Brighton with their deadly payloads.

Brenda had been scared the first time the air raid sirens had sounded their ominous wailing just after war had been declared in September. Back then she had been convinced that the entire Luftwaffe was about to demolish every last inch of Brighton. Nothing untoward had appeared in the sky over the town that time though. Dad had jokingly called the war the Bore War because nothing much happened at all for a long time apart from the rationing. Acquaintance with war had been informative. Even Brenda now knew the difference between Stuka, Dornier, Junkers or Heinkel bombers. There were pictures and silhouettes on posters, leaflets and cigarette cards. The latter had become a much wanted collector's item at school and as such a valuable trading commodity. All the boys – and even some of the girls – badgered their fathers and other male relatives for the cards. Brenda didn't have any herself; at home her little brother Eddie got Dad's cards but she knew them because Eddie badgered her to read the words on the cards to him. She always did. Eddie was only five years old and being his senior by four years meant that she had to help him out any way she could.

Deep zigzag trenches had been cut into the playground behind the school and the children piled in quite casually after noting the sky was devoid of the sight or sound of aircraft. The boys put on their gas masks immediately, half filling the trenches with otherworldly creatures that had strange snouts and large eyes which bulged sideways. The girls were slower, they hated the gas masks because most had shoulder length hair and found the gas masks a nightmare to get off. It was the only time that Brenda was pleased that her family couldn't afford to take her to a hairdresser's. Her mousy hair was much shorter on account of her basin hairstyle, so-called because a pudding basin was upturned and placed on her head every now and then after which Mum would snip off any hair that protruded below the rim. Brenda retrieved her gasmask from the rectangular carton box she carried it in and slipped it over her head.

During the first air raid warning at school it had taken the boys less than a minute to discover that their voices sounded oddly hollow in their new gas masks and that great fun could be had making funny noises in the masks. The teaching staff were oddly tolerant to the malarkey in the trenches, even when fart sounds had joined the repertoire. Brenda presumed that this was because they could all be torn into a thousand pieces for King and Country if and when the Luftwaffe did make an appearance one day. The trenches would be a death trap in the case of a direct hit she had overheard some teachers tell each other.

"We'll be buggered proper if Jerry knows what he is doing," one of the boys near Brenda said.

She frowned; she had ended up in a part of the trench where her form bordered that of older children. Brenda didn't quite know what 'buggered' meant but she was sure it wasn't polite language. The boy had dark hair but his face was already hidden by his gas mask. He was talking to another lad who had a basin hairstyle just like Brenda, though his hair was almost golden.

Brenda recognized them then. The dark haired one was Jamie, his family lived just a few doors away from her own. The other one was his mate Will, the two were usually inseparable. She shouldn't have really liked them for they were always finding ways of getting in trouble but they sometimes let Eddie play in their games and that was nice.

"That fancy Roedean School for girls has proper ones, I heard." Will answered. "Deep ones girdled with steel like the inside of the rocket ships in the pictures. We ought to sneak in one day and have a peek, Jamie."

Brenda crossed her eyes; one advantage of the gasmasks was that nobody could see your facial expression very well and it seemed the only suitable response for the idiocy of boys. They weren't going to take Eddie along on that expedition, she would see to it.

"What if there's an air raid?" Jamie asked. "We'd be stuck in them tunnels with a bunch of girls, Will. Hours on end. We'll both go bloody daft."

"True," Will answered. "Girls are silly."

Brenda glared at them both. She was standing quite close to them but they hadn't noticed it was her.

"Bbbrrrpppffftttt." Jamie blew a raspberry in his mask and within seconds their trench sounded like all the boys suffered from a collective attack of dysentery. Brenda joined the other girls in shaking her head in exasperation. She suspected that one or two girls happily joined in as it was difficult to tell who was making what specific noise when so many were at it. Classes had grown somewhat with the induction of evacuee children from London and some of those could be quite rude, or so Brenda thought. The teacher in charge of this section of the trench, Mr. Burchell, shook his head too but made no attempt to stop the fun.

Brenda smiled beneath her mask; the trench games were more fun than lessons and in a way the rude noises were funny. Her smile faded though when she registered the distant drone of plane engines and the pupils became quiet as eyes turned skywards. Some of the more timid children hugged the trench walls. The seagulls wheeling above the school screamed collectively in response to the strange sound of aeroplane engines coming closer at low altitude.

Perhaps a few of the gulls were also startled by the trench which presented an odd sight as hundreds of gas-masked faces were turned upwards. The strange robotic faces looked left and right. They sought to spot the incoming aircraft but it was as if they were shaking a desperate 'no' to whatever danger might be preying on them in the clouds overhead.

When the drone developed into a roar that drowned out the seagulls the nay-saying stopped. Everybody crouched down and made themselves as small as possible. Brenda pressed her side against the trench wall and pulled her knees up to the ventilator of her mask. She hoped Eddie would be alright.

3. SUSSEX BY THE SEA

The source of the roaring plane engines came into sight as four Lysander Mk2s passed overhead just as the single tone all-clear signal sounded.

"Coastal patrol," Will told Jamie happily, "They're our lads!"

The boys ripped off their masks and cheered collectively for their heroes high up in the sky while most of the girls started the dreadful struggle to disentangle their hair from the masks' clutches. The pupils clambered out of the trenches to line up in their forms and enter the school again whilst the teachers huddled around the Headmaster who was talking to them urgently.

Will and Jamie found their seats and fidgeted impatiently. Then Mr. Burchell stepped into the classroom with a wide smile on his face. This hitherto never observed deviation hushed the class in an instant; all the pupils stared at him in great expectation, even forgetting to rise to their feet as a sign of respect for the teacher's entry. This flagrant violation was noted by Mr. Burchell who gave a brief frown but then decided his news was far more important and his smile came back.

"Listen carefully boys and girls," he announced. "There has been an event of tremendous importance."

There was a collective intake of breath, even though Mr. Burchell's smile indicated the news was good.

"It's the British Expeditionary Force. The last troops have been evacuated from Dunkirk and are now back on English soil!"

The class stood, rising to their feet in an instant and cheering loudly, a collective whoop of relief and pride that was echoed from surrounding classrooms.

"Rule Britannia!" Jamie shouted.

"Now, now!" Mr. Burchell laughed. He waved the children down into their seats again. "It's not a victory. We escaped the jaws of defeat though. Apparently a great number of private vessels sailed to Dunkirk too, to help with the evacuation. You will be proud to know, I trust, that there were many brave Sussex skippers involved."

The class cheered again.

"*Sussex wun't be druv!*" Will hollered happily.

"Indeed it won't young Maskall," Mr. Burchell acknowledged. "*Sussex wun't be druv*, not even by that despicable dictator in Berlin. This is a moment to rejoice, albeit briefly, the war is far from over. I suggest that that we all stand and sing a heartfelt *Sussex by the Sea*."

The class rose as one and Will had never heard a more heartfelt rendition of the song, even though most of the boys –himself included- aimed for quantity rather than quality of sound as they sang the rousing marching song.

For we're the men from Sussex,
Sussex by the Sea.
We plough and sow and reap and mow,
and useful men are we;
and when you go to Sussex,
whoever you may be,
you may tell them all
that we stand or fall for Sussex by the Sea!

"Now," Mr. Burchell beamed when they were done. "A number of you will be awaiting news from relatives in the BEF. The Headmaster has decreed you may all have the rest of the day off."

This announcement raised the loudest cheer yet even though there were only two hours to go till the end of the day. All decorum was blatantly ignored as most pupils shouted, laughed and pushed each other in their haste to exit the school before anybody could change their mind about the unexpected freedom. A few looked concerned. Had any men remained behind? Did the expected battle take place?
Will and Jamie had no immediate relatives serving in the army and they relished in the moment.

It was Tuesday, June 4, 1940 and in Will's world, all was as well as could be.

4. GREY FLUFF

Mum didn't look very happy when Brenda and Eddie came home from school early. She looked tired and haggard and greeted them with a curt: "I still need to go to the shops."

"Shops!" Eddie nodded enthusiastically.

Mum sighed and Brenda knew why; it would take her twice as long to go shopping with Eddie in tow but Eddie looked really eager.

"I'll come and mind Eddie, Mum," Brenda offered. She would do her homework later, usually it was the first thing she did when she came back from school.

Mum shot Brenda a grateful look, "Are you sure you don't mind, dear?"

Brenda was pleased that Mum asked. It was at these moments that she felt Mum was aware that her daughter was in charge of Eddie an awful lot and that made everything alright. "Not at all. We can play the reading game, can't we, Eddie?"

"Shops!" Eddie repeated happily.

The reading game was very simple. Eddie pointed at things with letters and Brenda would read them out. Eddie had recently become fascinated with letters, which was probably because Brenda read a lot of stories to him. Eddie's favourite reading book was *The House at Pooh Corner* which he liked just a bit more than *Winnie-the-Pooh* because Tigger was in it and Tigger was Eddie's favourite character. Brenda liked

Kanga best because she had an inkling what it was like to keep an eye out for Baby Roo jumping around all the time.

Eddie clutched Brenda's hand while they followed their mum down towards the direction of Kemptown to go to Edward Street. There were a lot of shops there. Before the war Brenda used to go alone. Whenever her mum needed just one or two items from the shops she would have sent Brenda. All on her own, proudly clutching sixpence or a shilling as she relished the grown-up task her mum trusted her with. She also liked the freedom of roaming the streets free of supervision and the way some of the shop owners, who had come to recognize her, treated her with the deference they used for all of their customers. That made her feel grown-up too. The increasing air raid warnings had curtailed her independence, Mum was worried about safety on the streets now and Brenda secretly felt a little piqued that her sole task on these shopping errands was minding Eddie. The Luftwaffe never showed anyway.

It wasn't that she minded Eddie's company. Every time she looked down to see her little brother scurrying to keep up she would give him a warm smile. Mum had made him a cowboy suit for his birthday using a potato sack she had obtained from their grocer and on which she had sewn strips of an old blanket. Brenda had supplied an old hat she had bargained for at the Harper & Sharpe second hand shop as well as two gull feathers she had found on the beach near the Palace Pier. Dad had completed the gift with a revolver he had carved out from a piece of wood. It took a great deal more coaxing to get Eddie out of his cowboy suit and into his pyjamas since he had received these gifts, so taken was he by the gifts.

Brenda kept a sharp eye out on him when he would go outside to play because Eddie was now the envy of Sussex Street and Brenda was afraid some of the older boys might try to trick her brother out of his hat or even steal his toy gun. Not Jamie and Will, they were nice to Eddie, but some of the others might. She was quite sure Eddie would be inconsolable and much as she loved her little brother with his inquisitive blue eyes and fair curly hair she would be the one who would have to deal with that.

Brenda sighed.

"Whatsmatter?" Eddie asked looking up at her. "Do the letters hurt?"

"Letters? Hurt?" Brenda was confused.

Eddie pointed his toy gun at the shop signs which started to predominate the street.

"Letters everywhere," he clarified. "Does it hurt?"

"To read? No you silly Moppet."

Eddie pointed at the next store. "What's that sign say?"

"Stop. Here. For. Brighton. Rock," Brenda spoke slowly as she read the signs.

"Mummy," Eddie cried out and Mum turned around with a surprised look.

"What is it Edward?"

"Stop here for rocks!" Eddie answered.

"We haven't got time to stop now Edward, Mum is in a hurry," Mum answered.

Eddie pouted, "But Brenda said we should stop."

Mum glanced at the sweets on display in the window of the confectionary and frowned at Brenda. "Stop filling his head with nonsense, Brenda. We're not buying sweets."

"But…" Brenda started to object but Mum had turned around again. Brenda rolled her eyes. Eeyore was right when he said that some people had no brain at all, instead they had grey fluff that blew in there by mistake. Mum wasn't always like that but sometimes she did behave like it. Eddie pointed at another sign.

"Morris Sausage and Steak House," Brenda read out.

"There?"

"Twyner Fishmongers."

"There are no fish," Eddie noted. "Is the sea empty?"

"No Moppet, it's because of the war, there is less fishing. You have to come early now if you want to buy fish."

The early bird catches the fish. Brenda smiled, she liked that.

She duly read out the names of the Madeira Fruit Stores (*Pick of the Market!*), a Marks and Spencer Bazaar and countless other names indicating butchers, bakers, chemists and greengrocers till they reached the general store where Mum liked to do her shopping. Brenda let Eddie pull her along the shelves so Mum could be free to focus on the shopping she wanted. This had become considerably more complicated since the war started and Brenda could see Mum mumble, frown and run her index finger along the squares printed in the ration books. She felt sorry for Mum.

Eddie discovered letters on the labels of tins, jars, bottles and boxes of the products on offer. A new game was invented on the spot. Brenda read out the names of products which had letters which drew his attention: Scott's Porage Oats, Coleman's Vitacup, Bird's Puddena, Richereme Blancmange Powder, Hartley's Table Jelly, My Lady Bartlett Tinned Pears, Chivers Peas, Saxa Salt, Fray Bentos Corned Beef, Bisc-o'-Rye, Beefex Cubes and Huntley and Palmers Empire Assorted Biscuits. It all sounded awfully important when the names were read solemnly and out loud and Brenda liked this game.

"Do you know what it means?" Eddie asked, he pointed along the shelves. "All of it?"

"Yes, I do," Brenda nodded.

"Clever, clever Brenda!"

Brenda nodded her agreement. She certainly wasn't a dullard, she liked to know things and find out more about them. She didn't mind going to school like some of the children, sometimes she even liked it because a few of the teachers knew how to hold a class spellbound and they told lots of interesting things.

"Are there shops that sell letters?" Eddie asked pensively, running his finger along a complicated label with a lot of letters on it.

"A lot of them! Bookshops, sign-painters and offices full of people who do nothing but type letters all day."

Eddie nodded but then lost interest and pulled Brenda towards the counter. Mum was next in line to be helped by the assistant and Eddie was enthralled by the mechanics of this. When Mum handed over her money the assistant put it and the bill she wrote out in a small cylindrical wood pot which she attached to a trolley above her head. The assistant then pulled a cord and a spring sent the money pot whizzing on overhead wires to the cashier's office. She then crossed out some squares in Mum's ration book and by the time she was done the pot came sailing back with Mum's change in it.

Eddie aimed his toy gun at the pot as it came closer. "BANG!"

Mum was embarrassed and shot Brenda a look.

Brenda quickly took Eddie's hand and coaxed him out of the shop. They stepped into the sunshine outside. A cool breeze was blowing in from the sea, it held a light hint of brine and Brenda breathed in deeply. She liked the sea. It was always there, just like the seagulls always sailing over the rooftops.

"We can go to a letter-shop now!" Eddie told her.

"We have to go home, Moppet, so I can help Mum cook tea. You want to eat, don't you?"

Eddie rubbed his tummy and nodded. "Tigger after?"

Brenda smiled and nodded. She would take Eddie on another journey to the Hundred-Acre-Wood quite happily. She wondered if honey was rationed there. Poor Pooh-Bear wouldn't like that at all.

5. PENNIES & MUTOSCOPES

Will and Jamie wandered to the seafront and lingered on the promenade throwing wistful looks at the West and Palace Piers.

Will had rather enjoyed most of the war so far. There were bad things of course such as the food situation. Like most healthy twelve-year-old Brighton lads he held the *Führer* personally responsible for forcing Britain to introduce rationing. Will's family was poor and had never been accustomed to a well-filled larder but the current limitations caused by 'Nazi Nastiness' had sufficed to give him a perpetual feeling of hunger. Even worse, though sweets hadn't been rationed yet the sweet shops had noticeably diminishing supplies and much less on offer. He was also supposed to carry his gas mask everywhere and was forever losing it. That meant he often had to go to the Town Hall to apply for a replacement and that would earn him a good scolding on account of his failure to support the war effort.

Then there were the sleepless nights. Air raid warnings had started to pick up from March onwards again. Sometimes there would be welcome breaks from lessons at school but at nights it was worse. Gaffer refused to go to the nearest bomb shelter where many of their neighbours sheltered collectively. He said he would prefer to die at home and there was no telling where the bombs would fall at any rate. On those nights Will's family would move into the cellar of the small terraced house on Ashton Street and it would be hard to sleep soundly.

As far as Will was concerned the damned Nazis had a lot to answer for.

However, the war had offered a fair number of advantages as well. One of them was that a lot of men had left for the war, making it far easier for young lads to find the odd job here and there. Will and Jamie would roam the town in their spare time and usually managed to earn a penny here and a ha'penny there helping to unload goods from lorries for shop owners and running errands left, right and centre. In that process they had also expanded their stomping grounds; crossing the Boundary Passage to add Hove to their home ground of central Brighton and Kemptown.

On good days they even had enough coins to jingle them in the pockets of their shorts. They had used this day's extended free afternoon to go door-to-door to collect old newspapers and they had sold these to a fish and chip shop on the seafront for the usual penny a pound. They had got a bag of scraps to boot and walked along King's Road, on the sea side of course, happily nibbling at the bits of fried batter which had crumbled off in the fryers but still tasted of fish somewhat. It was almost like the real thing.

"Such a bleeding shame," Will indicated the West Pier.

Jamie nodded morosely. He knew exactly what Will meant.

Bereft of their more abled-bodied staff the arcade machines on West Pier had been practically unattended, meaning that Will and Jamie had been able to spend some of their newly earned gains on the *What the Butler Saw* mutoscopes. A penny allowed you to turn the hand-crank of these mechanical contraptions and hundreds of photographs would flick by so fast it was like watching a film at the pictures. These particular mutoscopes gave the impression that you were peeping through a keyhole as you pressed your eyes to the viewer. Beyond that keyhole you'd see a voluptuous young lady undress; revealing a buttock before dressing again, or a bare back with the tantalizing side swell of an actual boob. Will and Jamie had agreed that one of the mutoscopes must contain the Holy Grail of mutoscopic voyeurism, namely the combination of buttock and boob swell in one shot, and they had embarked on an ambitious quest to locate it by checking out all the *What the Butler Saw* machines when finances permitted.

A couple of the lads at school had boasted that some of the evacuee girls from London were quite willing to reveal bits and pieces in exchange for a penny or sweets. However, Will and Jamie had reckoned the mutoscopes were far more educational. Besides, the London girls they knew at school were bold and audacious; in other words, kind of frightening. The mutoscope girls just smiled enticingly or looked suitably mysterious. Nor did they complain if the lads turned the hand-cranks deliberately slow to prolong their penny's worth of fascination.

Hitler had put an end to these springtime delights. In May both piers had been closed as a precaution and the skies over London had been free of a Luftwaffe presence for so long that most of the evacuees had been returned home. Robbed of his chance to see both buttock and boob in one go Will had spent a few days cursing the Nazis and regretted once again that he was too young to join up so that he could teach them a lesson or two.

Accepting that the mutoscopes were well out of their reach the boys drifted through the maze of narrow streets in the Lanes and ended up in Norman's Milk Bar on Duke Street where Jamie treated Will to a milkshake. Jamie's dad was a furniture maker with a small shop on Sussex Street, between

Carlton Hill and Albion Hill, close to where Will lived on Ashton Street. Jamie's parents weren't very well to do but Jamie was never short of anything and he wasn't at all concerned about sharing with his best mate. Will liked Norman's Milk Bar but felt out of place, he was the only one there with a basin haircut. The style, if it could be called that, was considered indicative of poverty and sometimes joked about by the children who were better off. Not really in a way that was intended to be particularly nasty, adults were far quicker to discriminate him because of his background but the taunts made Will feel ashamed none-the-less.

Life would have been easier for him and Mum if his father had still been around.

The boys stopped by a sweet shop on the way home and laid down a penny for mint humbugs which they chomped during their walk along North Street, St James Street, and then George Street. Will knew they could walk the streets of Brighton blind-folded for the boys had conducted a smashing experiment on a recent Sunday. Will had worn a blindfold all the way from Albion Hill to Kemptown and then on to Hove. He had led the way and not along the Marine Parade and King's Road by the seafront, that would have been too simple. He had used the back roads and as many twittens as he could. These were the narrow alleys which criss-crossed the town. The best were the cat's creeps, the steep stairway alleys that connected streets at different height levels, so-called because they were the sneaky routes preferred by cats, small boys and folk who might not necessarily want to be seen whilst they went about their business.

Parts of Brighton were a veritable maze and the boys liked to go twittening through the alleyways. Jamie let Will give the directions and was there to prevent major mishaps, especially when they had to cross or traverse a length of street with traffic on it. Jamie had led the way back along an alternative route and the boys had considered the experiment a great success. In their minds it was important to know these sort of things.

The striped humbugs were finished by the time they crossed Edward Street to enter John's Street and the warren of streets around Carlton Hill and Albion Hill. They said goodbye at the end of Nelson Street, Jamie walking onto Sussex Street where he lived and Will having to traverse another two streets before he reached his home.

6. ASHTON STREET

Will walked around the back. His dad had died from an illness when Will had been very young and Mum had moved back into her parents' house. Will's grandfather owned a tailor workshop which occupied the ground floor of the small terraced house. Gaffer was the only employee and earned just about enough to get by. Everybody in the house – Will, Mum, Gaffer and Gran – used the back entrance to get in and out of the house. The front door was for customers.

The small back yard contained an outhouse and there was also a tin bath there which was brought in on Saturdays so everybody could have a bath. There was something resembling a kitchen in the cellar and a living room and bedroom on the first floor. Gaffer and Gran slept in the bedroom. At night two thin mattresses were brought in to the living room from the bedroom where they were stored in daytime and Will and Mum would sleep on those.

On the nights that they spent in the cellar, not knowing if Jerry was coming and even less certain about whether Jerry would bring bombs or parachutists if he did come, Gaffer would sit on the cellar stairs in his long johns, his Brody helmet on his head and a shotgun in his hand. Gaffer had been a soldier. As a young man he had served in the Boer War in faraway South Africa. He volunteered again as soon as the Great War broke out but was initially considered too old. When lack of manpower became acute he was accepted into a labour battalion and had worked on the narrow-gauge railways which served as a vital supply channel for the front line troops.

"The Huns were most impatient," he had once told Will. "They would never wait for us to repair damaged tracks before blowing them into smithereens again. They knew the routes see, at least segments of it and there was almost continuous artillery fire. And that was where us older and more infirmed blokes were sent to with a shovel, wrench, bag of bolts and spare rails. Not tucked away safely in some comfy trench like the younger lads."

It had been a rare moment. Gaffer stayed silent on the subject of his wartime experiences most of the time and Will remembered every word of the few references Gaffer sometimes made. It was enough for Will to reckon Gaffer was a war hero at any rate; something he wouldn't mind becoming himself. He'd return and there would be a victory parade for him. Will would walk next to the Major and people would throw flowers; Brighton would be at his feet and offer him a lifetime of free sweets.

Everybody was in the living room when Will walked in. The heavy blackout curtains were still open because it was still light outside. Mum was grateful when Will gave her a penny; he always gave half his earnings to her, knowing she had to work hard to make ends meet.

For tea Mum and Gran had performed their usual miracle with the meagre resources at their disposal because of the rationing. They had made what they called 'Mock Duck' with potatoes, sausage meat and a little sage. Will had never eaten duck before so he couldn't compare it but he enjoyed every bite of the meal and wished there was more.

Talk of the rescue at Dunkirk dominated the meal. Of late the news from France had caused an increasing sense of morose gloom in Brighton and Will had not been immune to this. He had been quite bewildered by the notion that Britain might be losing the war, in his universe the Empire bested all comers and it was simply unaccountable that Englishmen could be defeated by foreigners. However, many of the adults had taken to shaking their heads in resignation when the war was mentioned.

Will and Jamie had started to read the old newspapers they collected before bringing them to the fish and chip shops. Perusing these for articles on the war had made their grasp of the geography of Northern France sufficient enough to have been shocked when they read that Abbeville had fallen prey to the Nazis. Though the papers had focused on the brave efforts the Tommies were putting up - giving the Jerries a bloody nose for every inch of French soil that was fought over - the place names mentioned in the reports had suggested that the British Expeditionary Force was being encircled and their French allies driven back along the entire Western front.

Things had got worse when it became clear that the BEF had indeed been surrounded at a place called Dunkirk where the poor Tommies were pounded by Jerry artillery and Stuka bombers. It seemed that it was only a matter of time before the dreaded Jerry tanks started ripping their way through the final defences. If that had happened Britain would have been left without an army and Churchill -for all his tenacious belligerence which Will admired so much- would be forced to seek peace. Will had been outraged by the many adults who shrugged this away. He understood that it would perhaps be better to leave the strange foreigners of the Continent to their own devices. However, to accept defeat at the hands of the Jerries was more than his young patriotic heart could stand.

Gaffer suggested they listen to the radio after tea. Generally he distrusted London sources and preferred to hear the latest news at the pub. Or so he said. Gran teased Gaffer endlessly by reminding him that the news he heard at the Lion & Unicorn most probably came from London anyways. Gaffer would just shrug and head to the Blue House —as the locals called the pub- to have his pint of Cloudy and Black. On a good night he'd listen to George Harding and his brothers play music there and the festive mood would entice him to have a glass of Merrydown as well. Jamie's dad would sometimes go with him, but neither man spent all their free time there like many in the neighbourhood did.

§ § § § § §

The BBC radio presenter gave his listeners more details about Operation Dynamo, including descriptions of the hellish conditions at Dunkirk. Then he mentioned Prime Minister Churchill's speech. Winnie had been defiant to say the least, it was clear he intended Britain to fight on just as he had promised in an earlier speech. Only this time he indicated that this fight might well take place on English soil.

The presenter read out a part of the speech:

We shall go on to the end. We shall fight in France, we shall fight on the seas and oceans, we shall fight with growing confidence and growing strength in the air, we shall defend our island, whatever the cost may be. We shall fight on the beaches, we shall fight on the landing grounds, we shall fight in the fields and in the streets, we shall fight in the hills; we shall never surrender.

"Bloody hell!" Will exclaimed with admiration. None of the adults admonished him for his language use, they just nodded and straightened their backs somewhat.

"The beaches," Gaffer said pensively. "That will include our Sussex beaches. Never thought I'd find myself in the front line again."

7. THE LONE REDCOAT

Brenda and Eddie came home from school and found Mum fast asleep on the sofa, still wearing her nurse's uniform. She worked at the Royal Sussex County Hospital. Brenda whispered to Eddie that he had to be very quiet, drew the curtains shut and unfolded a blanket which she spread over Mum. Then she ushered Eddie out into the hallway and out of the front door. She had a ha'penny and there were some shops which sold ha'penny sweet bags. An expedition to a sweet shop would entertain Eddie for a while as Dad was working a late shift. If she met him by the gate of the workshops he'd understand and pick up some chips on the way home; fish if they were lucky but these days you had to be early if your mind was set on a battered cod or haddock. Then they would go home and Dad would wake Mum and Brenda would set the table and divide the spoils from the chippie.

"Is Mum ill?" Eddie stretched his neck to look back at the drawn curtains of the front window.

"No, Moppet, don't worry," Brenda answered.

"Whatsmatter?" Eddie frowned.

Brenda screwed up her face in thought. She always disliked it when adults sought to conceal the truth with vague assurances or reverted to 'when you're older'. In the latter case she always asked how old she would be and she kept a secret list, neatly organised by the promised ages. A few years more and she could start producing the list on her birthdays and demand the delayed explanations.

She knew what the matter was but had no idea how to convey that to a five-year-old whose interpretation of things she told him often left her puzzled. Mum's shifts could be hard and recently they had been especially so. Her brother George was in the BEF in France and it had been weeks since they had heard anything from him. The newspapers spoke of triumph and bravery; courage under fire. The ward Mum worked in had been sent two dozen wounded men from the evacuation and they spoke of chaos and disorganisation; it had been every man for himself, some had said, amidst that hell of exploding shells and shrieking dive bombers. It was hard work as it was but the wounded soldiers' tales had fed Mum's imagination with regard to the fate of Uncle George who was still missing.

Mum hadn't told Brenda this. She had gleaned it from conversations between her parents in the evenings after Eddie had been ushered into bed. Brenda understood enough of it to be extra nice to Mum when she came home from work in a state of exhaustion. She decided that she would explain it to Eddie when he was older.

"Nothing's the matter, Eddie," she smiled brightly. "Mum's just tired, Moppet. Shall we go to the sweet shop?"

"Sweets!" Eddie nodded, easily distracted by the thought of multi-coloured sweetness in big jars.

§ § § § § §

The Redcoat looked left and right, clutching his gun. The palaces looked peaceful; their stately decorated domes, towers and minarets looked elegant even in the light of a dull overcast sky. The Redcoat was wary though, he knew that the Tipu Sultan wasn't called the Tiger of Mysore for no reason.

There could be any number of traps laid out in the gardens surrounded by the pavilions of the Sultan's exotic pleasure palaces.

The British soldier dashed from behind the cover of a tree to make towards nearby bushes but just then two turbaned Mysore guards charged him wildly; waving their weapons in the air and howling like wild men.

"Bang!" The Redcoat fired his pistol at one of the guards who took a tumble and started rolling around clutching his belly in pain.

"Bang!" The other guard screamed his pain as he clutched his injured shoulder, while at the same time still coming forwards to deal with the Redcoat.

"Bang! Bang!" The wounded guard fell backwards; eyes bulging and throat rattling as he thudded against the ground where his body shook convulsively before it became still.

The Redcoat blew imaginary smoke from the barrel of his pistol and then laughed when the two Mysore guards rose from the dead and assaulted him anew; only to be punctured by the bullets which the Redcoat never seemed to run out of.

Brenda sighed. She sat on a bench with her back to the Brighton Dome and facing the Royal Pavilion which the boys were using as a backdrop for their game of Tipu Sultan. Will and Jamie wore tea towels around their head as turbans and Brenda's red coat had been appropriated for Eddie to wear. There didn't seem to be much point to the game other than that Eddie repeatedly killed Will and Jamie who made a great show of dying with noisy drama before getting up to do it all over again.

Eddie was utterly delighted with the game, though, and it kept his mind off Mum at home. It also helped pass the time till they could meet Dad at the end of his shift so Brenda decided to bear the cold she felt without her coat. She hadn't really been happy when her coat had been acquisitioned for the battle but it had seemed a good compromise because the initial intention had been to tie her to a Mughal column as a captured Indian Princess in need of rescue. Brenda had told them 'no' using some of the language Will and Jamie liked to use and they had been very impressed. She just hoped Eddie wouldn't repeat it in front of Mum or else she'd be in a world of trouble. In the meantime, she had to admit that the theatrical performances of Will and Jamie were secretly amusing. She didn't know whether or not it was alright to think so when she thought of her missing uncle George in France. The war was confusing sometimes; the papers were full of it, but looking around the Royal Pavilion gardens with the cries of seagulls and soft rumble of traffic in her ears the war seemed far away.

8. RAZOR THIN SLICES OF MARS

Will and Jamie had gone to the top of Richmond Street, close to the highest point of Albion Hill. Richmond Street had the steepest gradient of the whole town and there was a vital experiment to be conducted. The lads both laid their tubular gas mask containers on the road surface and on the count of three they gave it a push. The containers started rolling down the hill, slow at first but then gathering speed and Will and Jamie soon had to run to keep up with them, shouting loud encouragement at their respective containers and occasionally interceding when the containers started to veer off course.

The aim was to see how far down Richmond Street the containers would roll and, of course, to see which one would go the furthest. Will and Jamie had both bet a penny so the winner was assured a handsome profit. The game was very rudely stopped by a grumpy Air Raid Precaution Warden who used his feet to bring both containers to a halt first and then seized the boys by the ear lobe, one lad's ear in each hand. He pulled them up so far that Will and Jamie had to stand on their toes to keep contact with the ground. They squirmed at first till they realised the Warden wasn't going to let go and they were just increasing their own discomfort. They settled into the indignity of being held up by the ear like a small child. The Warden gave them a stern sermon about safety on the streets and risking the breakage of valuable property which might one day save their lives.

When he was done he snorted and let go of their ears. Rubbing the painful appendages the boys picked up their containers and slunk off sheepishly, much to the amusement of bystanders who had stopped to watch the scene. However,

Will and Jamie hadn't meant to sabotage the war effort as suggested by the Warden, they had simply been genuinely interested in the results of their experiment.

"We'd better take out the gas masks next time," Will summed up what he had learned from the experience.

"We could put in some marbles," Jamie brightened. "That would make a fine noise!"

"What do we do with the pennies?" Will asked, it was inconceivable that they could put them away till the experiment could be resumed another day. Pennies were meant to be spent, particularly now that the town's supply of sweets seemed to be increasingly diminishing. Will loved the sweet shops and newsagents where large glass jars that held four-and-a-half pounds of sweets formed long rows upon shelf after shelf; filled with every colour of the rainbow and augmented by other displays of chocolate treats.

Sherbet, liquorice, boy blue cream whirls, jelly beans gobstoppers, acid drops, mint humbugs, aniseed balls, black jack chews, fruit gums, pear drops, bull's eyes, brandy balls, glacier mints, chocolate drops, Callard & Bowser butterscotch, Sharps toffees dolly mixture, honeycomb, fudge, toffees, and many more.

Will knew them all and he and Jamie updated their knowledge of sweet stocks, prices and quality in their immediate surrounding of Albion Hill, Carlton Hill and Queen's Park but also Kemptown at the bottom of the hills by the eastern seafront, the Lanes in the centre of town and the Hove to the west.

To their alarm they had noticed that there was not a glass jar left that was filled to the brim as it ought to be. Levels were descending steadily and the rarer a sweet became the more children seemed intent on acquiring a sample for a goodbye taste. There were a lot of sweet goodbyes these days.

"Penny's worth of sweets each and then share them?" Jamie suggested and Will grinned. Jamie and he tended to have the same mind on the things that really mattered.

The visit to the nearest sweet shop supplied them with aniseed balls and black jack chews. Jamie had some extra coins as usual and went into a newsagent close to his home, coming out with a Mars bar.

Will's eyes grew wide.

"I've been trying to find those everywhere, thought they'd run out completely!"

"Under the counter," Jamie winked. "My Dad is repairing some furniture for them."

They took their bounty to Jamie's house, one of the terraced houses along the steep incline of Sussex Street. Unlike Will, Jamie had his own room and decent things in it too. Stacks of Beano and Eagle comics for one but also some neat toys. Jamie's dad had made him wooden models of a Supermarine Spitfire and a Hawker Hurricane. They were big, needed a whole hand to hold them and Jamie and his dad had very carefully painted the models in some detail. Will's favourite was the Spitfire and he held the model to fly over his head every now and then while he read Beano magazines. His favourite character was Frosty McNab, especially since the latest editions had become suitably warlike and involved

Frosty McNab taking on the Wehrmacht. Most of the Beano characters were very good at outsmarting Nazi thugs.

While Will was reading Jamie had fetched his dad's razor blade and was slicing the Mars bar into very thin wafers. Will looked at him questioningly.

"I heard someone at school talk about it," Jamie said happily. "Make a Mars last a whole week like this."

Will nodded admiringly and accepted one of the wafer thin slices with relish. He let the chocolate melt on his tongue and relished the caramel. Jamie had finished his slice much faster and decided that his hoard wouldn't be too diminished if they had one more slice each. Another exception was made after that and it was hardly worth keeping the rest so they ate those too. Then serious attention was paid to the sweets. These were vastly entertaining. The aniseed balls made their tongues go bright red and the black jack chews, which also tasted of aniseed, turned their tongues black. Will and Jamie had hoped they could continue to switch colours but soon the colours merged into dark brown goo on their tongues. Some on their lips too and a bit on chin and cheek to boot and that caused new mirth.

"The Spitfire is the best plane," Will declared, flying the model in a tight circle around his head once again. He loved the distinctive shape of the Spitfire; there was something sleek and elegant about it. The Messerschmitt 109 looked like a lethal brute, sure enough, but somehow the Spitfire managed to convey a form of cunning which the Jerry planes missed. It had the best engine too as far as Will was concerned.

"It'll beat the Messerschmitt Bf110, sure," Jamie conceded. "But the Bf109 is better higher up and there's less chance of the engine cutting out in sharp turns."

There followed a complicated debate about the merits of the various planes which lasted until Jamie's father stuck his head around the corner.

"Good afternoon gents," he said jovially.

"Good afternoon Mr. Hall." Will said politely. He was very fond of Jamie's dad; the man was forever planning outings and never seemed to even consider omitting Will from his father-son activities with Jamie. Jamie's mum called them 'The Terrible Trio'.

"How did you enter my kingdom?" Jamie challenged his dad.

"In a rocket-ship of my own design," Mr. Hall answered grinning. He spotted his razor. "If I catch you playing with my razor again, Jamie, I'll give you a clout around the ears."

Jamie stuck out his discoloured tongue.

"Very handsome," his dad conceded. "Don't let your mother see and wash your faces, you're not little boys anymore. Listen gents, I have a proposal in mind."

Will grinned happily, whenever Mr. Hall used those words fun was bound to follow. He fondly recalled an outing Mr. Hall had arranged to the Bertram Mills Circus the previous summer. It had left him with two lasting impressions. The first of a football match played by elephants and the second of a group of female performers in show outfits which had left him feeling oddly funny.

More often than not though, Mr. Hall's proposals involved going to the pictures. Mr. Hall was a great fan of the pictures and since the year had started he had already treated Jamie and Will to viewings of *Pinocchio*, *The Lion has Wings*, *Stagecoach*, *Band Wagon*, dozens of matinee episodes of *Flash Gordon* and *Buck Rogers* and no less than two visits to Max Miller's *Hoots Mon!*

Max Miller was a Brightonian and loudly proud of that and Will and the two Halls considered him to be the best comedian in Britain, though Mrs. Hall thought Miller was a bit too risqué for the lads. Truth be told Will could sense Miller was skirting the edge of decency sometimes by the reactions from the audience but the contents of those jokes left him puzzled. It was like adults spoke a language of their own sometimes.

He had asked Gaffer about one of the jokes once. It had been in a theatre show at the Hippodrome where Miller, dressed in his usual brightly coloured gaudy suit, had produced his famous 'blue-book' and read out:

A Yorkshire man came to London and he couldn't get any Yorkshire pudding . . . so he went home and battered himself to death.

Will had heard it repeated again and again on the streets that week but had no clue as to why it was considered so funny. When he cited it to Gaffer the old man had first chuckled and then guffawed before ruffling Will's hair and telling him he'd understand one day as well as forbidding Will to repeat it in the presence of the womenfolk in the house.

There would be no renewed acquaintance with Miller or other heroes of the silver screen this time though. **Mr. Hall** had other plans.

"I thought we might catch the bus out to Devil's Dyke tomorrow, go for a bit of a wander along the Downs," Mr Hall said. "Maybe have some practise if we see a nice field for it."

"Bring the catapults?" Will began to beam.

"Are you sure this thing will work?" Jamie quoted Flash Gordon.

"I have experimented with models," Mr. Hall replied in something resembling Dr. Zarkoff's voice. He turned to Will. "You'll talk to your mother about it?"

"I will," Will nodded though everybody knew she would say yes, she was always rather pleased that Will was able to go on some adventure or other in the company of Mr. Hall.

"Very good. Put the razor back, wash your faces and then carry on as you were, gentlemen," Mr. Hall said.

"TTFN," Jamie said.

"Pardon me?" Mr. Hall looked puzzled.

"Tat-Ta For Now," Jamie looked disappointed. "From ITMA!"

"It's That Man Again," Will provided helpfully. "On the radio."

"I don't know how you two manage to keep track of all that but find it impossible to memorise your school subjects." Mr. Hall laughed and left.

9. WINKLING WINKLES

Mum's parents had received word from the army. Uncle George had been wounded and was now a Prisoner of War in a German camp somewhere. Mum took the bus to Rodmell that weekend to be with her parents who were distraught.

A neighbour had watched Eddie on Saturday afternoon and Brenda had gone shopping all on her own, with the family's ration books and two whole shillings. The neighbour had helped her make tea for when Dad got home from work. It was a simple affair, drawn from one of the many rationing recipes that were popping up but Dad had made a show of enjoying the meal and complimented Brenda on her cooking skills.

She beamed, she had never been in charge of the house like this before and she was very pleased that Dad had acknowledged this milestone by thanking her just like he always thanked Mum for her meals.

"Since we're going to be on our own tomorrow," Dad said. "Perhaps we can go on an adventure?"

"Yes!" Eddie bobbed up and down.

Brenda was filled with anticipation but also worried that he would not get his rest. Dad worked long hours too and was often tired. He solved her concerns though, when he continued speaking.

"Some fresh air will do me good," he winked at Brenda as if he had read her thoughts. "I've been told they are going to close the Undercliff Walk next week because they are fortifying it against the Jerries. I thought it might be a nice idea to walk to Rottingdean and back while we still can? Collect some winkles while we are there?"

Brenda's eyes grew wide. With no immediate worries to attend to anymore it would be grand to go on an outing and she always enjoyed it when Dad set time apart to spend with his family. He was very good about it and always made it special.

"Winkling would be very nice," she smiled.

§ § § § § §

They set out early in the morning, heading towards the Marine Parade. It wasn't very busy on the beaches yet although it was promising to be a beautiful day and Brenda was in good spirits.

They walked east along the shingle beaches and groynes and on to Black Rock and then the Undercliff Walk along the bottom of the chalk cliffs. Brighton Council had built a seawall here that ran all the way to Saltdean some four miles away. The seawall protected the cliffs from erosion and the Undercliff Walk ran over the seawall rather than over a beach.

The three of them had walked here before, Mum usually came too, and Brenda liked it a great deal. Walking on the seawall was like walking along a battlement, especially when the tide would come in and sent spray flying over parts of the walk. Dad always turned that into a game, hoisting Eddie on his neck, waiting for the wave to recede and then running past before the next wave thundered in.

The cliffs to their left had been reworked when the seawall had been built, scraped clean of all irregularities so they looked unnaturally regular and flat and they glared in the sunlight. It was impossible to look at the cliffs for too long though it was temping. Not only because of the many bird nests but also because the hundreds of flint nodules which protruded from the chalk.

"It hardly seems necessary to fortify this place," Dad remarked, "It's like a fortress already. I suspect they'll add barbed wire and mines. Gun emplacements and pillboxes on the cliff tops, maybe."

"England is strong though, isn't it?" Brenda asked.

Dad shook his head. "Most of the army's equipment was left behind at Dunkirk. Right now I do believe the First Canadian Division is the strongest army on British soil until we sort ourselves out again."

Brenda was pleased, he seemed to have forgotten that she was just a nine-year-old girl for a moment and was talking to her like he was having a chat with a friend. She said proudly: "We have the Royal Navy. And the Royal Air Force!"

"Spitfire!" Eddie grinned and made engine noises.

"Yes we do, but Herr Hitler has the Wehrmacht. If Jerry comes..." Dad's voice trailed off.

"Dad? Do you think the Germans will invade?" Brenda asked worriedly.

Dad was silent for a moment as he looked over the broad expanse of the sea.

"I hope they don't," he said at last.

Brenda recognized that he avoided a direct answer to her question. That probably meant that he did think they would invade but didn't want her to worry.

"We'll stop them if they do," she said hopefully.

"But at what cost?" Dad asked with a sad smile. "Brighton has already paid a high price."

Brenda considered that for a moment. The flotilla which had been sent to Dunkirk to help evacuate the troops still seemed like a miracle but over the last few days it had become clear to Brightonians that it had come with a price attached.

Two local pleasure steamers had been sunk, the *Brighton Queen* and the *Brighton Belle*. Smaller vessels, both pleasure boats and fishing-craft, had also been lost; *Our Doris, Mary Joyce, Royal Rose, Sea Flower, Cornsack, Four Winds* and *Flower of the Fleet* would never return to their home port again. The names had been buzzing around the streets and in the pubs as folk in Brighton tried to assess the new realities of the war. A girl in Brenda's class had lost her grandfather and a cousin when their fishing boat was strafed by German planes.

They paused by the Ovingdean Gap where they wandered onto the shingle beach and then on to the chalk bedrock where the low tide revealed a fascinating landscape of canyons and valleys containing rock pools.

The rock pools were enchanting, filled with all sorts of creatures. Small fish and crabs of all sizes peered from beneath the seaweed and kelp they used for cover. Here and there a starfish clung to the rock or small shrimps moved to and fro. The pool floors were covered with molluscs, barnacles, limpets and anemones.

After a while all three began to collect winkles. They had brought spare socks which were perfectly suited to hold the captured little molluscs in large numbers. Dad would leave them in the bucket overnight, sprinkled with salt to make the creatures spit out sand or dirt and then he would boil them. After that followed the rewarding task of using a pin to extract the winkles from their shells so they could be eaten.

"Time to winkle out them winkles," Dad would always say.

Collecting them was easy and they soon had all of their spare socks filled. They retired back to the shingle beach and rested with their backs against the seawall, enjoying the day's warm sunshine. Dad opened the large satchel he had been carrying to reveal various delights. He had managed to obtain a Fry's Five Boys milk chocolate bar for Brenda and Eddie as well as a bottle of Thomas & Evans Corona fizzy drink. Brenda and Eddie shared the chocolate and the drink. The Corona was limeade flavour. Eddie was fascinated with the bottle top. It had a special stopper attached to a metal bracket so it could be popped open and resealed and he happily opened and closed the stopper a million times, the metal bracket clicking against the bottle as he did so.

Dad had got himself a bottle of Pale Ale and a portion of jellied eels for he was very fond of them.

When they were done they continued on to Rottingdean where Dad insisted on walking to the windmill first. The mill was constructed of blackened wood and stood on a hill a little ways out of the village which it seemed to be guarding like some glowering monolithic giant.

"Very well," Dad said when they had walked around the windmill. "Time for a cream tea."

A cream tea was an integral element of the Undercliff Walk and Brenda's favourite part. They walked down into the fold of land which funnelled down to the beach and went to the High Street. The proprietress of Dad's favourite tea rooms was a jolly white-haired woman who reminded Brenda of the fairy godmothers in the fairy tales. She brought a large tray and Brenda's mouth watered at the sight of the scones. The walk had given her a healthy appetite even though she had already had half a chocolate bar for herself, a rare treat as it was.

The proprietress really was like a fairy godmother, she distributed plates with scones, small jam and butter bowls, little teapots, sugar bowls, milk jugs and cutlery with magical speed and dexterity. All the tableware matched and Brenda beamed, cream tea in Rottingdean always looked so festive. She always felt they were celebrating something.

She caught Dad looking at her and realised he was enjoying her reaction. Her ability to glean information from parental conversations she overheard in the evenings meant that Brenda knew family outings were special. Both Mum and Dad would put a little bit aside for weeks on end to save for a luxury like this. Dad would even skip his weekly pub evening to save coins. She gave him a warm smile and he returned it. It was one of those rare moments and she relished it. Dad was usually sparse with his emotions.

"No cream!" Eddie frowned.

"It's because of the war," Brenda told him. She glanced at the butter which was very pale. The fairy godmother caught her look.

"Margarine is the best I can do today, love," the fairy godmother shrugged. "But it's premium brand margarine, not that stuff with so-called marine oils."

"Fish-oil," Brenda wrinkled up her nose.

"I don't want fish-oil!" Eddie declared.

"There's no fish-oil in this, Edward." Dad said. "Don't worry, this is good."

"Good," Eddie nodded solemnly.

"Vitamin A and D in there too," the proprietress added.

"Then we won't have to have our spoonful of Cod Liver Oil and Malt tonight, will we Dad?" Brenda asked hopefully. Mum held the stuff in high regard as a vitamin supplement for the ration diets but Brenda hated the thick treacly stuff with a passion.

Dad held up his hands. "I am not going to get between your mum and her Cod Liver Oil, not for all the money in the world."

Brenda nodded, that was quite sensible of him. "Tell us about the smugglers?"

He always did, and it was always the same story but that didn't matter. Brenda liked the gleam in his eye and the passion in his voice when he related the Rottingdean days when sailing ships would moor offshore in the very early morning and sailors would row smaller craft to the beach to deliver brandy, tobacco and lace. Sometimes the Revenue Officers would show up and boys who acted as runners would dash down from their lookout points around the village to inform the smugglers that the law was on its way. The High Street had a maze of connected cellars where the contraband would be hidden ere the sun rose or else a string of ponies would be waiting to carry the goods inland across the downs.

"Jungle Book song," Eddie demanded.

"That's right, Edward, the writer lived here in Rottingdean for a while," Dad nodded, pleased that Eddie had remembered. "He wrote about the smugglers. Not in the Jungle Book though."

Dad started reciting the poem which had become part of their cream tea ritual.

If you wake at midnight,
And hear a horse's feet,
Don't go drawing back the blind,
Or looking in the street.
Them that asks no questions
isn't told a lie
Watch the wall my darling
while the gentlemen go by!

Brenda joined in, she knew Rudyard Kipling's 'Smuggler's Song' by heart.

Five and twenty ponies,
Trotting through the dark-
Brandy for the Parson
Baccy for the Clerk.
Laces for a Lady
Letters for a spy

And watch the wall my darling
While the gentlemen go by!

They walked back to Brighton after the cream tea. The tide was coming in but hadn't advanced far enough yet to launch an assault on the seawall, though that didn't dampen their spirits.

"Well thank you, children," Dad said happily. "It's been good to be here before it's all taken away from us for a while."

"No, Dad, thank *you*!" Brenda said. It had been a grand day, it was hard to believe there was a war on. "Sussex is pretty, isn't it?"

"That it is," Dad said and then recited a few lines from another poem.

I'm just in love with all these three,
The Weald an' the Marsh an' the Down countrie;
No I don't know which I love the most,
The Weald or the Marsh or the white chalk coast!

Brenda had no such problems making up her mind, she would choose the Downs and chalk cliffs every time. They probably didn't even have cream tea in the northern forests and eastern marshes.

§ § § § § §

Will and Jamie had spent the day by the sea. They had first headed to the rock pools past Black Rock. There they had decided that the ridges and gullies looked like the surface of the planet Mongo. They had jumped from foothold to foothold with their arms outstretched, making mechanical buzzing sounds as they piloted Zarkov's rocket-ship over Mongo's surface. Foes had been easy to find for the young rocket-ship cadets as some of the rock pools held big green crabs. These cranky creatures snapped at pointing fingers with their pinchers and it was a good trick to try and anticipate their attack so the offending finger could be pulled away just in the nick of time.

"It'd be a right cracker if one of us walked into the Royal Sussex County Hospital with one of these buggers clinging to his hand," Jamie said.

Will nodded. "And refused to let go. Perhaps you should try it."

"Might lose a finger," Jamie said thoughtfully as he eyed a particularly grumpy crab. "How would I pick my nose?"

Eventually they lost interest in the game and meandered west again along Madeira Drive. Although the beaches were not as busy as they should be in the summer there were still a fair few people about. Mostly young men and women, presumably the young men were soldiers on leave trying to make the most of life while they still could.

Although the courtship game between men and women was mostly incomprehensible for Will even he could sense that there was an urgency in the abandonment of the usual etiquette. Destruction and death lay around the corner and none begrudged those who would bear the brunt of the fighting a last carefree flirtation and a passionate kiss on the beach.

Will and Jamie were mesmerised by two comely and giggly girls who darted around a handsome young man in swimming trunks like carefree butterflies whilst he tried to grab them in a game of tag that was almost like a dance. Further on couples were kissing though Will didn't really understand the appeal of that unless it was a novel way to swap sweets. He did have an eye for the shapely curves in the ladies bathing costumes though and enviously suspected some of the lucky soldiers might see a buttock and the side swell of a boob before the day was up. Maybe he should get a uniform.

By the time they reached Banjo Groyne and the Volks Railway Halfway Station and viaduct Will was feeling oddly giddy. They started ascending the long stairs up the Eastern Terrace and Will began to hum a song. Jamie recognized the tune and started singing and Will joined in.

Gertie was a good girl
Till the day that she met me
Gertie was refined
But liked to show her dignity.

"Race you!" Jamie shouted halfway up and they started running, still singing as loudly as they could.

I told her that I loved her
Then I asked her for a kiss
When I whispered in her ear
What happened then was this

They reached the top of the stairs simultaneously, practically out of breath but still competing to sing the loudest.

She said she wouldn't
I had an idea that she would!
She said she shouldn't

But I told her that she should!

Several people passing by frowned. A man with two young children guided them across the road away from the boys. Will grinned, now he felt like a pirate, in contempt of civilised society. He wheezed as he took a deep breath to complete the song as boisterously as he could. As always Jamie was on the same level and Will could tell that he too enjoyed being churlish for a bit.

§ § § § § §

She said she couldn't
Because she wanted to be good!
She said she wouldn't
I thought perhaps she would!!

The boys sang it really loud and Dad frowned as he directed Brenda and Eddie across the road. Brenda's eyes widened as she recognized Will and Jamie just before the boys headed in the direction of Palace Pier, turning their backs on the cream tea expedition before Eddie recognized them.

"I swear, Brenda," Dad growled. "If you ever bring boys like that home I'll boot them out of the house."

"I won't," Brenda promised, though she was puzzled as to why on earth she would want to bring a boy home. Boys were idiots.

"It'll be a while yet, I suppose," Dad said mysteriously and laughed.

Brenda nodded. She wondered if she could devise a plan to keep Eddie from becoming an idiot too. She hoped idiocy wasn't contagious because then he might have already caught it from Will and Jamie. That would be a real shame.

10. A FAREWELL TO BANJO GROYNE

The Jerries had entered Paris and the French were seeking an armistice. The news was not unexpected but had an impact nonetheless. Nazi Germany now dominated the continent, from Poland to France and the Low Countries to Denmark and Norway. The realisation that Britain now stood alone, like David facing Goliath, hit home hard. Streets, schools and pubs were abuzz with heated debates. Would it not be better to accept an armistice with the Jerries as the best possible outcome to the war? Let that raving lunatic in Berlin have his way in Europe? After all, Britain still had the Empire and that Empire should be their focus, not continental squabbles. Others, still remembering Chamberlain's sacrifice of the Czechs shook their heads. When had Hitler ever been content with his gains? More; the madcap dictator always wanted more.

The Prime Minister gave a speech in the House of Commons and then repeated it for a radio broadcast. He reminded the populace that the situation was dire but by no means hopeless, for the Royal Navy and Royal Air Force would greatly hinder if not defeat a German attempt to invade.

"....if we fail, then the whole world, including the United States, including all that we have known and cared for, will sink into the abyss of a new Dark Age made more sinister, and perhaps more protracted, by the lights of perverted science. Let us therefore brace ourselves to our duties, and so bear ourselves that, if the British Empire and its Commonwealth last for a thousand years, men will still say, 'This was their finest hour.' "

§ § § § § §

First the piers, now the beaches were being closed. Will went to the Kemptown seafront to see for himself. He stood on Marine Parade and looked down at Madeira Drive. He had always viewed Brighton's seafront on both sides of the Palace Pier -basically all of King's Road and the Marine Parade- as a vast playground designed to keep him entertained and amused.

He stared desolately at Banjo Groyne; his favourite place in all of Brighton. The sea defence stretched beyond the shingle beaches on either side of it, broad enough to hold a parapetted walkway and its round end had always seemed like a grim bastion tower to Will.

If he stood there facing the sea during the best high tides it was like standing on the bow of a ship, clutching on to the ship's side whilst the waves bashed the stone wall of the tough groyne, causing almost continuous sprays of salty water to descend on the viewing platform. Will and Jamie would then imagine themselves to be on a man-of-war. Buffeted by wind and briny spray they would stagger around as if trying to keep their footing on a heaving deck. All the while they would shout and sometimes use their catapults to dispatch French frigates or Spanish Galleons to the bottom of the sea.

Banjo Groyne was also a good place to fish, or pretend to be fishing whilst looking wide-eyed at the girls in their bathing suits playing beach cricket on a nice summer's day. Or else just chuckle at the out-of-town visitors trying to negotiate the pebbles as they attempted to reach the sea, especially if they did so barefoot. Locals had no problem with the shingle and would often forget that this was an acquired skill till they were reminded of it again by the sight of struggling out-of-towners on the shingle beaches.

Turning around on Banjo Groyne was just as good. The grey cliffs towering over Madeira Drive looked like town walls defending the riches of the elegant Regency terraces which rose above them in the stately manner of palaces. The view made Will feel like one of the king's archers in the days of King Arthur; bravely defending one of the outmost defences of Camelot whilst the besieged inhabitants shouted encouragement at him from the inner town walls. On other days it was Dr. Huer's Hidden City which needed to be protected from the likes of Killer Kane. The beach kindly provided sound effects for that because the sea would hiss and the pebbles rattle as a spent wave withdrew again.

Walking towards the Palace Pier along the Madeira Drive was to his liking too. Magnus Volk's electric railway ran overhead here, supported by sturdy stilts and Will and Jamie like to throw pebbles —easily attainable on a shingle beach- at the wheels and underside of the trains as they passed right over the boys whilst they devised ingenious plans to derail a train there one day. Then there were the long colonnades along Madeira Drive which Will liked as well. There were places where it reminded him of a Roman arena. His mind would see the public cheering in the space behind the colonnade, on the colonnade walkway and up on the Marine Parade; no less than three tiers of Romans applauding their bravest gladiator. Will would wave up at the majestic little Victorian lift tower, which rose above the street level of the higher placed Marine Parade and protruded outwards from the cliff side; for surely it was from that regal structure that the Emperor of Rome would have watched the arena below. Will had very fond memories too of being part of the mass of people who came to watch the cars and motorcycles during the annual Brighton Speed Trials. It was sheer exhilaration to watch the vehicles perform their timed run down Madeira Drive, roaring past at top speed.

The boys had built a box car a few years ago, intending to take it down to Madeira Drive for a speed trial of their own but the steep incline of Richmond Street had proved more tempting. The maiden voyage of the box car had been its only one. The ride was eye-poppingly breathtaking but the box car had ended in a splintered wreck, Jamie had broken an arm and Will had suffered a concussion.

Next time, they had sworn solemnly, they would build a better one and might include some sort of braking system.

The colonnades had been sandbagged now and Madeira Drive had been closed to the public. The upper reaches of the shingle beaches had been covered with uncountable rolls of vicious looking barbed wire and the lower stretch of the beaches now sported pyramid shaped blocks of concrete to deter tanks and anti-landing craft spikes. There were also numerous huge fuel tanks stacked up below the Aquarium which were to be rolled into the sea when the time came, hopefully to set the very water ablaze.

Will and Jamie had heard of Sefton Delmer's broadcasts for the BBC's German Service in which he provided useful English phrases for Wehrmacht soldiers.

Now, I will give you a verb that should come in useful. Again please repeat after me:
Ich brenne... I burn;
Du brennst... you burn;
Er brennt... he burns;
Wir brennen... we burn;

Ihr brennt... you are burning.
Sie brennen... they burn.
And if I may be allowed to suggest a phrase: 'Der SS-Sturmführer brennt auch ganz schön...' The SS Captain is also burning quite nicely.

When the church bells started ringing their alarm at the sight of German landing boats Will and Jamie were determined to rush towards the seaside with their catapults to lend the Home Guard a hand and hopefully to watch the sea catch fire. It would be a bittersweet moment, they knew, because the piers were unlikely to survive such an inferno, but that might be compensated by their heroic combat against any slightly scorched *SS-Sturmführers* who managed to make it to the beach.

Today Will had mixed feelings. On the one hand it had made no sense to him that the likes of the Undercliff Walk were being fortified whilst Brighton itself seemed undefended like a ripe plum ready for the picking. Up till now little had been done on the town's seafront with the exception of the placement of a few anti-aircraft guns. Now the place was bustling with activity. Vulnerable buildings on the sea front were evacuated, men were piling sand bags in front of some buildings and windows were being taped up with strips of linen in diamond patterns to lessen the dangers of flying glass. Another working party was removing the decking of the Palace Pier to render it useless as a landing platform for invading troops.

This all made sense to Will but it also felt as if a part of his very being had been taken away from him, his sense of space amputated. Moreover, he felt a cold chill close around his heart. These men surely believed that the Jerries would come. That they were not taking half measures was emphasized by a Police Constable who stopped to warn Will that the beaches were to be mined as well; under no condition were children to venture into the new defensive zone. Will nodded a silent acquiescence, feeling discouraged by the desolate view of his now heavily fortified and inaccessible personal fiefdom.

However, Will never stayed morose for too long, he had a natural tendency to bounce back and the sight of machine-gun posts and Oerlikon anti-aircraft guns being erected at improvised redoubts cheered him up. War was fascinating again and doubly so when a battery of two six-inch naval coast defence guns was positioned in front of Lewes Crescent. Will drank it all in, suspecting that it would not be long before someone figured out that it would be best to send the various civilians taking a curious stroll along the promenade back to their homes. There could be nothing more common-place in Brighton than that walk, especially in the summer, but already it seemed out of place; incongruous with what now looked like a war zone.

11. THE CANADIANS

The first Canadians of the Second Canadian Division started to arrive in small numbers. Units of the Royal Canadian Artillery who added their 40-mm Bofors AA Guns to the defensive positions along the sea front. They were housed in a number of large houses on Preston Road, opposite Preston Park, and Will and Jamie planned an expedition in the hope of catching a glimpse of the Canadians.

"Do you reckon they'll have face paint? Bows and arrows?" Will asked hopefully, as they made their way north to Preston Park.

"You think they're Red Indians?" Jamie asked.

"Well, they might be," Will shrugged.

"Don't be daft," Jamie laughed. "Red Indians live in the United States, not Canada. The Canadians have Mounties I think. They wear proper red coats, just like our army used to."

Somewhat to their disappointment the Canadians had neither red skins nor red coats. In fact, they looked an awful lot like regular British troops. Will and Jamie sauntered up to the low garden wall of one of the houses. There were a number of off-duty soldiers there who were happy to talk to them and when the Canadians opened their mouths Will and Jamie finally noticed a difference for the Canadians talked really funny, a bit like the actors in the pictures made across the Atlantic Ocean. They were also generous, giving the boys a large chunk of cheese each.

"We've seen your Bofors guns," Will said, his mouth still half full with cheese. "There's no way the Jerries will come close to Brighton now."

"I wouldn't be so sure of that kid," one of the soldiers sighed in his strange accent. "Most of the coastal positions are manned by the Local Defence Volunteers with a few regulars like us pitched in to beef the LDV up a bit."

"Yeah," a second said somewhat bitterly. "Thrown to the wolves I say. We're expected to slow the Germans down a bit, give them a bloody nose, but the real fighting will take place inland, that's where they hope to stop them, not here."

"Tom, what happened to careless talk costing lives?" The third soldier said cautiously.

"It's hardly a secret Justin," the one called Tom shrugged.

"Hey guys," the first soldier said to Will and Jamie. "Some of my uniform is busted and I am hopeless with needlework. Would you know anybody who could fix that?"

"David's right. We need laundry doing too," Justin added.

"I can arrange that for you," Will said quickly.

"Yeah, you know how to sew kid? You do laundry too?" Tom looked dubious.

"No, but my mum does, and my grandfather, he has a tailor shop," Will said. "And she...we could use bit of work to be honest."

Will avoided looking at Jamie as he said that. Jamie had been to Will's house a few times and knew his friend's family was poor but it wasn't something they talked about. There was an unspoken agreement that Jamie's house was by far the best place to muck about in because he had his own room and the best toys. Jamie was also always very diplomatic about the boys' own income. He knew that Will liked to give his mum some of his earnings and never accused his friend of spending less on their leisurely interests, nor did he make a big fuss about spending just that bit more himself. Will suspected that Mr. and Mrs. Hall were also well aware of his situation. Whenever Mr. Hall planned an expedition Will's mum always insisted on giving Will what she could spare to give to Mr. Hall. Sometimes as little as tuppence but usually a shilling. Mr. Hall always closed Will's hand around the proffered money with a wink.

"Give it to your mother Will," he would always say and Will would do precisely that.

Once he could start working properly at fourteen he could help out his mum. This was Will's main ambition, driven by an obligation he felt towards the father he had never known. He'd be able to pay Mr. Hall back then too.

"The question is," Jamie said rather cheekily. "Can you pay?"

"You bet kid," Tom grinned. "Sugar, butter, tinned fruit, Golden Syrup. Some idiot pen-pusher at HQ made a fortunate miscalculation. Reckoned there were ten times as many of us here."

Will's eyes grew wide; Mum would be absolutely delighted.

"We'll need to sort out an exchange rate," Justin added. "Can you bring your mother here?"

Will nodded happily. He suspected that she would assign some tasks to him, like wringing out the laundry but the sort of payment the Canadians were offering was fast becoming worth more than money so he'd quite happily help her out.

12. 'R' FOR RESCUE

Brenda heard the front door open and knew Dad was home. She carefully put away Margaret Elizabeth, her large doll with a porcelain head dressed in an old-fashioned gown. It was her prized possession. Her eyes widened as Dad came into the living room. He was wearing a clean dark blue boiler suit and wore a blue armband with 'Civil Defence' printed on it in yellow letters. He also had a tin hat which had been painted black with a white 'R' on it. He looked incredibly proud.

"Oh Charles," Mum just shook her head sadly. When Dad sat down Eddie was all over him, feeling the armband and reaching for the helmet.

"Daddy is a soldier!" Eddie said.

He squealed as Dad picked him up and held Eddie in the air for a moment before settling the boy on his lap. Brenda bit her lip. Dad used to do that with her when she was little but he had stopped doing it a long time ago and sometimes she wished he hadn't.

"Not quite, I am in the ARP now, Edward," Dad said.

"A soldier," Eddie nodded. "Brenda, letter!"

Brenda followed his pointing finger and she read out the white letter on the helmet. "It's an 'R'. What does it stand for Dad?"

"Rescue," he answered solemnly. "In case people get trapped in bombed buildings."

"You'll get them out?" Brenda asked.

"Yes, and put them on a stretcher and then bring them to your mum at the County Hospital."

"You'll spend most of your time patrolling the streets to see if anybody's light is showing," Mum shrugged.

"Watch duty," Dad nodded. "Two hours an evening."

"Can I come?" Eddie asked.

"It's too dangerous," Dad answered.

"Dangerous," Eddie mused. Then he scrambled off Dad's lap and went to a corner of the living room.

"Well, I am proud of you!" Brenda declared.

"Thank you Brenda," he replied with a foolish grin.

Eddie came back. He was holding his wood pistol. He gave it a regretful look, then handed it to Dad. "For you. When it is dangerous."

Dad looked at the proffered toy and threw Brenda a look. She nodded, *take it.*

"Thank you very much, Edward," Dad said gravely, and took the pistol as carefully as if it had been a real weapon. "I shall carry this with me when I am on duty."

"Daddy is safe now," Eddie replied with a satisfied look. "Safe from dangerous."

Brenda hid a smile.

13. DOGFIGHT!

Will was at Jamie's house listening to the radio with Jamie in the living room. His mouth hung open in a rather undignified way; all thoughts of sweets, pennies, rocket-ships and mutoscopes banished from his mind. All he was aware of were bright white cliffs topped by England's green and pleasant land and a vast expanse of bright blue sky filled with aircraft.

Will and Jamie had been listening to war news when a BBC war correspondent had stopped reading his script. It had been about a small convoy sailing into the Straits of Dover and the radio crew were observing it from the top of the iconic White Cliffs of Dover.

All of a sudden the correspondent had started speaking faster and more urgently. The convoy was being attacked by the Jerries even as the correspondent watched.

"And...there you can hear our anti-aircraft going at them now. There are one, two, three, four, five, six – there are about ten German machines dive-bombing the British convoy, which is just out to sea in the Channel."

Jamie's mouth had also dropped open. News reports were dry and dignified; this one was unlike any they ever heard before. They could hear noises in the background; other men talking and what sounded like gunfire.

"Here they come. The Germans are coming in an absolute steep dive, and you can see their bombs actually leave the

machines and come into the water. You can hear our guns going like anything now."

Will held his breath. He could see it all as if the Hall's living room had been transformed into the Kemptown Odeon cinema.

"Anything interesting?" Mr. Hall stuck his head around the door, holding his pipe in one hand and a newspaper in the other. "Lads?"

"The Jerries are attacking," Jamie said with surprise in his voice.

"Good Lord, has it begun?" Mr. Hall strode to the window as if he half expected to see a Jerry tank growling its way up the steep incline of Sussex Street. "I thought we'd hear commotion at sea first."

"No Mr. Hall," Will said. "On the radio. They're attacking a convoy in the Dover Straits."

"Now the British fighters are coming up."

Will clenched his fist.

"Now we'll show Jerry what we're made of," Jamie grinned.

"This is happening now?" Mr. Hall came closer, his face showing the same wonder Will and Jamie felt.

"I can hear machine gunfire. Oh! Here's one coming down! There's one going down in flames! Somebody's hit a German

and he's coming down with a long streak, coming down completely out of control!"

Will and Jamie cheered, throwing fists into the air.

"Good Lord!" Mr. Hall said.

"And now...the pilot's bailed out by parachute. It's a Junkers 87, and he's going slap into the sea...and there he goes. SMASH."

Will and Jamie cheered again. This time Mr. Hall joined them.

"Now, then...oh...there's a terrific mix-up over the Channel!! It's impossible to tell which are our machines and which are Germans...there's a fight going on, and you can hear the little rattles of machine gun bullets."

Will saw the whole scene unfolding before his eyes; the Jerry airman clutching the lines of his parachute as he watched his burning aeroplane plummet into the sea. He was probably cursing like the Jerries in the Beano, Air Ace and Eagle comics. Gott im himmel. Donner und wetter! That sort of thing. Then looking up at the dog fight taking place over his head where the graceful Spitfires circled in a dance of death around the stricken Jerry planes.

"There's another bomb dropping. Yes. It has dropped. It has missed the convoy! You know, they haven't hit the convoy in all of this."

"Good!" Mr. Hall exclaimed.

"The sky is absolutely patterned with bursts of anti-aircraft fire, and the sea is covered with smoke where the bombs have burst. Oh yes, I can see one, two, three, four, five, six, seven, eight, nine, ten Germans haring back towards France now for all they can go – and here are our Spitfires coming after them."

This was like listening to a football match on the radio with the home team now on the counter, both teams dashing in the direction of the opponent's goal.

"Of course, there are a lot more German machines up there. Can you see, Cyril?" The correspondent asked someone.

"Yes, there are one, two, three, four, five, six, seven on the top layer, one, two, three – there's two layers of German machines," Cyril answered. *"They are all, I think, I could not swear to it, but they were all Junkers 87's."*

"There are two more parachutists?" The correspondent asked somebody else.

"No, I think they are seagulls," another voice answered.

Mr. Hall laughed at that. He motioned for Jamie to get out of his chair and sat down next to the radio. Jamie settled on the floor with Will.

"Oh, there's another fight going on, away up, now! I think about 20, 25, or even 30,000 feet above our heads… the anti-aircraft guns have put up one, two, three, four, five, six bursts. There we go again…What?...Oh…we have just hit a Messerschmitt. Oh that was beautiful!"

"Hurrah for the RAF!" Will shouted.

"He's coming right down. I think it was definitely that burst got him. Yes, he's come down...Oh; he's coming down like a rocket now. An absolute steep dive."

"Welcome to England Jerry. Ha!" Jamie's eyes were wide.

"There's another! There's another Messerschmitt. I don't know whether he's down or whether he's trying to get out of the anti-aircraft fire...There's a Spitfire! Oh, there are about four fighters up there...One, two, three, four, five fighters fighting right over our heads. Now there's one coming right down on the tail of what I think is a Messerschmitt and I think it's a Spitfire behind him. OH, DARN!! They've turned away and I can't see. I can't see."

"Bloody hell!" Mr. Hall said completely forgetting there were children in the room.

"Hullo, there are one, two, three; and – look! There's a dog fight going on up there! There are four, five, six machines wheeling and turning around. Now, hark at the machine guns going! Hark! One, two, three, four, five, six; now there's something coming right down on the tail of another."

Will was seeing it from a Spitfire cockpit now, a complex technical contraption in which all he had to understand were the controls of the machine guns.

"Here they come; yes, they are being chased home – and how they are being chased home! There are three Spitfires chasing

three Messerschmitts now. Oh, boy! Look at them going! Oh, look how the Messerschmitts..."

Will released a burst of fire at the fleeing Messerschmitts.

"Oh boy! That was really grand! There's a Spitfire behind the first two. He will get them. Oh, yes. Oh, boy! I've never seen anything so good as this! The RAF fighters have really got these boys taped. Our machine is catching up the Messerschmitt now."

Will increased his speed by turning what looked like a mutoscope's crank-handle.

"He's catching it up! He's got the legs of it...now right in the sights!"

Will pressed a knob and watched his eight machine guns pump out trails of bullets at the Messerschmitt.

"Machine guns are going like anything. No, there's another fight going on. No. they've chased him right out to sea...I can't see, but I think the odds would be certainly on that first Messerschmitt catching it! Where? Where? I can't see them at all..."

"Just on the left," another voice said. *"See it?"*

"Oh, yes, oh yes. I see it. Yes. They've got him down too...Yes, he's pulled away...Yes, I think that first Messerschmitt has been crashed on the coast of France all right."

"Just doing me job Guv," Will said, satisfied with this day's work. "Part and parcel of being an RAF pilot."

Will didn't notice Mr. Hall grinning away at him.

14. THE TIN HAT

Will and Jamie felt like rich men when they left the Southdown Bus and Coach station near Queen's Park. A number of bus drivers had paid them to fetch cups of tea or sweep out the buses and both of them felt the satisfaction that accompanies having a pocketful of coins. Jamie spotted a confectionary store which still stocked chocolate and invested in a Kit Kat which he split with Will.

They took the remainder of their fortune to Harper & Sharpe, so-called on account of the fading sign on the front of the two story building at the far end of a mews on St James Avenue; *Harper & Sharpe, Corn & Forage Merchants.* Harper & Sharpe, however, had long ceased trading in hay, straw, chaff and oats and the building was now occupied by a business the owner liked to call Blake's Emporium. Everybody else called it Harper & Sharpe on account of that old sign.

As far as Will and Jamie were concerned the store was a treasure trove. Mr. Blake sold second-hand goods but you couldn't really tell that from the outside of the building. The two paned windows on either side of the door were dusty and filled with cobwebs and shadows. Will pushed open the door and the boys went in. There were rickety shelves, cupboards and tables that formed a veritable maze within the shop which occupied the entire ground floor of the building. Every available surface was cluttered with the flotsam and jetsam of Brighton; piles upon piles of junk amidst which a clever lad could discover treasures if he took the time to explore all the nooks and crannies properly.

"Here Will, look at this," Jamie had discovered an old brass microscope which he was eying up with bright eyes but Will wasn't paying attention. He was examining one of the corners of the shop. It was crammed full with assorted odds and ends but his eye had been caught by one specific item. He picked it up with reverence; it was a tin hat, just like the Tommy helmet Gaffer had. It seemed old and a bit battered due to multiple dents in the wide brim and scratches in the matte khaki paint but the liner on the inside was still intact, as was the chin strap. Will tried it on, it was just a bit too big for him but he figured that if he stuffed some old newspapers in it and fastened the chin-strap tight enough it would do.

He felt a sudden overwhelming need to own it, somewhat surprising himself with this feeling. He had coveted things before but those times it had been more of a daydream. Will and Jamie could spend ages in front of the window displays of the fancier toy shops in Kemptown which catered to well-off Brightonians or out-of-town visitors. There were usually amazing toys on display, from graceful toy sailing boats to ranks of brightly painted lead soldiers. Girl's stuff too, but they ignored those toys, preferring to look instead at the rows of colourful tin plate figures and vehicles or the Dinky Toys. They harboured no hopes of actually obtaining any of it; just pretending that you were playing with it was enough.

Jamie had nice toys at home because his father made them for him, mostly wooden lorries and cars detailed enough in the way they were made and painted to look far more realistic than the tin plate toys, just about as good as Dinky Toys Will reckoned. The two fighters Mr. Hall made marked both Jamie's change in interest and his father's progression in his toy making skills. Mr. Hall enjoyed it greatly and would often summon the lads to his work shed in their yard to show the progress he was making on this that or the other during his spare time. Jamie was lucky in that as most of the kids in Albion Hill simply played street games or constructed their own crude playthings, though most of the gaffers who didn't spend all of their time in the pubs could fashion a decent set of building blocks for their grandsons. Will had one of those home-made sets too as well as a bag of marbles to which Gran faithfully added a few on Will's birthdays and at Christmas. For the rest improvisation was a key word. If the boys encountered a stray length of rope which was long enough to be slung around one of the street lamp posts they could happily swing from it for hours and just about anything even vaguely round could reach breakneck speeds on the steep streets in Albion Hill.

It had been harder for the lads last summer when one of the shops in St James Street had suddenly displayed Buck Rogers rocket ships and a variety of Ray Guns. These had come all the way from America. Will and Jamie had gathered up the courage to go in to get a closer look but had been promptly sent out again by an ogre with long silver hair and glasses. She made quite clear that their likes weren't welcome in all of the town's establishments.

Jamie had been furious.

"It's not like I was going to bleeding steal anything," he had complained back at the house in Sussex Street.

"Some people equate class with trust," Mr. Hall had nodded. "It used to be a great deal worse when I was a lad before the War. We didn't have Ray Guns either but we made do."

The lads had grinned acceptance at that but had been very pleasantly surprised when they had been summoned to the work shed the week after that and were shown two fair sized sturdy hand catapults.

"Far better than Ray Guns," Mr. Hall had beamed proudly. "Hawthorn for Jamie, blackthorn for Will."

Their eyes had grown wide. Catapults like these were serious business. Mr. Hall had clearly thought so too.

"I talked to your gaffer and mum about this Will," he had said in the serious tone he sometimes reckoned even a playful father needed to employ. "They said you could have it if you stick to the rules I am about to lay down for the both you."

Will had nodded.

"I'll take you out to the Downs and teach you how to use these," Mr. Hall had said. "You're not to use them in town. If only one Brighton window — no matter how small — happens to shatter because you were being a nuisance then I will thrash you within an inch of your life. That counts for you too Will."

Will had nodded, oddly pleased that a grown-up man was prepared to give him a beating if he misbehaved. Mum sometimes lamented that Will could use a good smack. She was usually right as well, Will never meant to misbehave but he did get overtaken by his own boundless enthusiasm at times.

"We talked about trust last week lads. That shopkeeper might not trust you, but I do. Do you understand?" Mr. Hall had asked. "These catapults are a sign of that trust. I want your promise, as a man, that you'll behave sensibly with them."

Both Will and Jamie had straightened their backs and broadened their shoulders, filled with pride at this first initiation into manhood. They had already both been yearning for the day when they could exchange their shorts for long trousers, and this had been just as good, even better in a way.

Everybody had been so pleased all around that Mr. Hall had treated them to a visit to the Hot Pie Shop on St James Street.

Will loved it there. The shop exuded confident professionalism with its spotless counters and floors and the pastry cooks dressed in white busily rolling and pressing the pies on their pie presses. Will and Jamie had each ordered a four penny beano pie filled with a mixture of minced steak, baked beans, mashed potato and gravy and Mr. Hall had ordered his favourite minced steak pie. Though Mr. Hall had sternly told the boys to wait with eating till they were home he was the first to burn his lips when he succumbed to the odours drifting from the paper bag in his hands. Will and Jamie had to laugh and then tucked into their beano pies, nibbling small bites because they really were still too hot to eat properly. All had about half their pie left when they came back to Sussex Street.

Mr. Hall had kept his word and taught the boys to be proficient shots. He had also made himself a catapult after the first lesson on the Downs and that December he had taken them poaching on a moonlit evening. Will hadn't known if Mr. Hall had talked to Mum or Gaffer about that beforehand, Mrs. Hall was kept in ignorance at any rate. However, when Will had walked into the living room at Ashton Street late that evening and proudly presented his family with a small pheasant and a rabbit he had received nothing but praise. The lads kept their promise too and refrained from using the catapults in town, apart from the beach which they decided did not constitute part of the town proper.

Will turned the helmet in his hands. This was more than a toy, this was the war too. He really wanted it. He slowly walked to the front of the shop with the tin hat in his hands. Jamie saw what he was holding and fell in step.

Mr. Blake, unshaven and bleary-eyed, growled a greeting.

"How much does the helmet cost?" Will asked tentatively.

"Proper one that, Mark 1 model from 1916," Mr. Blake peered at the helmet. "The owner got himself one of those Zuckerman helmets, the new model for civilians. Dunno why, the steel they use for them is much weaker. These old ones offer much better protection. Not a bad idea in times like these. You can have it for a bob lad."

Will looked down at the helmet.

"How much did you make today Will?" Jamie asked him.

"Six pennies," Will answered downcast.

"I can give you thruppence Will," Jamie offered. He looked at Mr. Blake inquiringly. The shop owner was known to drive a hard bargain but something in Will's expression must have softened his heart for a moment.

"As an exception only lads, and don't you go telling your mates that I am getting soft in me old age," Mr. Blake growled. "Ninepence."

Jamie smiled but Will was still hesitant, it would be the first time he wouldn't share his earnings with Mum. She never asked him to but he knew she regarded the contributions Will made to the household money as a welcome extra. Mr. Blake sensed his hesitation and grew grumpy, assuming Will was trying to lower the price.

"I gave you thruppence off the asking price lad," he growled. "Ninepence. Going once…"

"Sold," Will made up his mind. The boys handed over their money and left the shop, Will clutching his precious helmet.

"You were worried about your mum?" Jamie asked.

Will nodded unhappily. He wanted to marvel at the helmet - his helmet- but felt a pang of guilt.

"Here mate," Jamie pressed another tuppence into Will's free hand.

"I thought that was all you had...back in the shop," Will was puzzled.

"I had more, but I wasn't going to tell him that was I?" Jamie grinned. "Give that to your mum Will."

"But how about you? You..."

"Will have to do without any more sweets today," Jamie shrugged. "The Hall-Maskall Austerity Drive. For King and Country."

"For King and Country," Will agreed. Those words always cheered him up. He pocketed the tuppence feeling awkward, Jamie had been a real mate today and Will didn't really know how to express his gratitude.

"Well, are you going to put that damn helmet on or what?" Jamie asked impatiently.

Will did so immediately and wore it all the way home. When they passed their local ARP station he gave the Warden on duty a prompt salute, unaware that passers-by were grinning at the sight of a boy in shorts wearing a Tommy helmet that was several sizes too big for him and kept on wobbling left and right.

§ § § § § §

The evening was marked by continual air raid warnings and Will helped Gaffer carry the bedding downstairs to the cellar where Mum and Gran were making tea. It was a simple stew with lots of carrots and mashed potatoes. The lack of meat was compensated by a lot of extra gravy powder and as a special treat there was grated cheese. Mum had taken a couple of mended uniforms back to the Canadians and they had given her a chunk of cheese on top of the payment of sugar and tinned fruit that had been agreed upon. She opened one of the tins for dessert, saving the other for another time. They were peaches, heavenly sweet, and everybody got two slices. Will tried to savour his as long as he could while Gaffer carefully poured equal measures of the juice in the tin into glasses. He mixed that with water and it made perfect lemonade as far as Will was concerned.

When it was time to sleep Gaffer took his accustomed place on the stairs; in his long johns, shotgun in his hand and wearing the Brodie helmet he had worn at the Somme. If the Nazis landed parachutists on Ashton Street that night to capture a tailor's workshop they would be in for a surprise when they entered the damp cellar.

Will put on his pyjamas, then strapped his own helmet on and went to sit next to his grandfather, armed with his blackthorn catapult and his bag of marbles for ammunition. He also had a bag of fine round pebbles which he had selected on the beach near Banjo Groyne but he reckoned any Nazi thug charging down the stairs deserved to be struck by Will's Class-A ammunition.

Mum looked at him and shook her head. She was about to say something, probably along the lines of it being a school night but Gaffer shook his head at her.

"Let the lad be," he said. "I'll need all the men I can get if Jerry comes tonight."

Will beamed.

"You two," Mum shook her head. "You might as well join the Local Defence Volunteers while you're at it."

She didn't know that both Gaffer and Will had made inquiries about the LDV but had been turned down because they had been respectively too old and too young.

That night Will fell asleep sitting on the stairs, his head resting on Gaffer's shoulder and his helmet so far askance that it almost hung completely sideways.

15. GUARDIAN ANGEL

The children were huddled in a corner of the little green patch which centred the small square. They were enthralled by a game of glarnies. Will and Jamie were taking on two other boys of their own age. They flipped the marbles with their first finger against their thumb and tried to land them in gullies formed by the partially exposed roots of a London planetree.

Brenda and Eddie looked on. Eddie clutched Brenda's hand and regarded the game with awe, marvelling at the intensity of the competition. Brenda didn't share his fascination, she admired the marbles instead. The twisted colour markings inside the glass spheres were pretty, just about the only bright things on this dull grey day.

"Hurrah," Eddie piped when the game was won and Brenda ruffled his fair curly hair. As always she envied his curls for a moment.

"Enough already?" The winner, Jamie, challenged the others. The two other boys pouted and drifted off. They weren't keen on losing more precious marbles to Jamie and Will.

Will adjusted his Brodie helmet. The tin hat was far too large for Will and forever wobbling around and sliding askew and he looked silly in it, Brenda thought. Will's bright blue eyes seemed to laugh as he watched the other lads drift away.

"That was good," Will said happily. "What next?"

"Sweets!" Eddie suggested and Will laughed.

"There aint many left," Jamie shrugged.

"Jamie is right," Will said wistfully. "Besides, I haven't got a penny right now."

"Neither do I," Jamie shrugged apologetically.

"Sweets," Eddie said with less conviction.

"I have a ha'penny," Brenda said. "Mrs. Parsons sells ha'penny portions."

Eddie, Will and Jamie brightened.

"Well done, Duck!" Jamie said.

"I am not a duck," Brenda frowned.

They left the square to go to Parsons Confectionary. The small shop had a narrow door and a display window filled with rows of sweet jars forming a kaleidoscope of bright colours. Mrs. Parsons welcomed them in, she was old but had bright emerald eyes and a kindly face framed by a mane of abundant hair with some traces of red fire still amidst the grey.

"Just a ha'penny, ma'am," Brenda said shyly, it felt like begging a little bit.

"Which will buy you a ha'penny of sweets," she answered with a warm smile.

"You can each taste one sweet each first if you'd like," the shopkeeper stated and the children shared glances of disbelief; this was unheard of.

"Are you sure?" Jamie asked carefully, not quite sure if they were dealing with a sane person.

"Positively," Mrs. Parsons smiled. Not only did she appear quite sane but she filled the space with a bright radiance, as if the sun had broken through the overcast sky outside and now danced upon the rainbows created by the jars. The delighted children drifted around the shop, running their hands along the jars and examining potential candidates more critically. They took a long time making their choices but Mrs Parsons did not seem to mind at all. She understood it wasn't easy. Instead she voiced the names of whatever sweets she saw them look at....there seemed to be no end to the heavenly delights.

The children waved happily at Mrs Parsons when at long last they departed, Brenda clutching a paper bag which held a far larger content than a ha'penny justified.

Seconds after stepping out onto the street there was a terrifying roar overhead and the air raid warning sirens began to wail. The children looked up to see a dog fight straight overhead and then the ground seemed to shake and a loud boom sounded from the square where they had been earlier. They looked at each other with open mouths and then ran around the corner.

The very corner of the little park where they had just been playing glarnies was now a churned mass of disturbed earth from which rose the back end of a Messerschmitt, the black and iron cross clearly visible on its rump and the swastika on its tail an odd sight in a Brighton Square. The front end of the plane seemed to have simply disappeared.

"LET'S GO!" Will began to run towards the plane, determined to beat the ARP wardens to the wreck.

Brenda held on to Eddie's hand as the little boy struggled to follow Will.

"Will, wait!" Jamie shouted.

Will looked back at Jamie curiously.

Jamie threw a pointed glance at Eddie and Will understood. Reluctantly he came walking back adjusting his helmet with an embarrassed grin on his face.

"Thank you, Jamie," Brenda said fervently. She had little desire to possibly see a dead German pilot, let alone let Eddie near one. She had heard Mum tell Dad stories about the war injuries she had treated often enough to know that it would be horrible.

She was surprised that Jamie had realised all of this but then he ruined it all by saying, "Duck has sweets, we mustn't leave her out of our sight."

"True," Will nodded.

"I am not a duck," Brenda said with exasperation.

"Sweets!" Eddie lost interest in the plane and Jamie winked at Brenda.

She felt bad for thinking the worst of him and held out the bag asking, "Anybody want a sweet?"

All three boys nodded and grinned.

16. THE FIRST RAID

It was a Monday morning and Will sat at the table in his pyjamas still feeling rather sleepy. Mum had already left for work which was why he was up so early. Though she always tried to be quiet in the morning Will usually woke up anyway. Mum's main job was at the public baths in Park Street. A lot of people didn't have bathrooms and those with a shilling to spare went to the public baths rather than limiting themselves to options at home which involved filling a tin bath tub. The shilling bought the use of a towel, a piece of soap and time in one of the huge bathtubs in a cubicle. Mum was one of the attendants who operated the hot and cold water taps outside the cubicles. Bathers would holler for more hot or cold water when they needed it and during busy periods Mum would be scurrying around trying to keep up with the demands. She always left so early in the morning because the work involved a lot of cleaning as well.

Will yawned, now that he was up he didn't really want to crawl back into bed but he was still too groggy to do much more than yawn. It was around six o'clock and it would be another half hour before Gran came out of her bedroom to boil water for a cup of tea. Will heard the sound of horse hooves and the light rumbling of wheels on the street outside, that would be the bread vendor starting his rounds with his bread cart. As the sound of the cart became more distant it blended with the rhythmic purring of aircraft engines. Will frowned but then decided it was probably an RAF coastal patrol; he should have heard the air raid warning warbling away like a mechanical banshee if it was the Luftwaffe.

He became wide awake when he suddenly heard the stuttering of an ack-ack gun as well as the louder and steadier crack of a Bofors gun. Brighton's defenders had opened fire and that could only mean one thing...

He gasped, Mum wouldn't have reached the public baths yet; she was out there on the streets.

"GAFFER! GRAN!"

Will ran to the chair next to his mattress where his clothes lay neatly folded, already pulling off his pyjama top. More ack-ack guns and at least one other Bofors gun joined in as the aeroplane's droning approached. Will shot into his clothes. There was still no air raid warning, but surely Mum would realise what the sound of the anti-aircraft batteries meant and find cover.

"GAFFER! GRA..."

Gaffer came storming out of the bedroom, shotgun in his hand. For just a moment Will visualised Gaffer in the middle of Ashton Street in his long johns, firing the shotgun into the air at the Jerry aeroplanes.

Gaffer suddenly seemed decades younger and fully alert. Will didn't have to explain what was happening; the old man took it all in within a fraction of a second.

"Will, stay away from the windows. Put on your gasmask and stay low, I'll fetch Gran and..."

A new sound was added to the cacophony outside, piercing whistles at some distance away.

"DOWN!" Gaffer shouted at Will and both dropped to the ground.

The whistling stopped abruptly, transforming into crumps and then the tremendous booms of explosions which followed each other in quick succession. The windows rattled in their frames and from his position on the floor Will saw dust jumping up as the floorboards trembled.

The explosions ceased and it seemed oddly quiet despite the continuation of the hum of aircraft engines and the fretting of the anti-aircraft guns. Only now did the incessant wailing of the air raid warning add its rising and falling pitch to the other noises.

Will put on his gasmask and then his helmet, padded now with old newspaper so that it didn't wobble so much. He made for the stairs.

"Will!" Gaffer hollered after him. "Come back here."

Will was already at the backdoor and with surprising speed Gaffer bounded down the stairs and then through the little yard where he apprehended his grandson by the gate; grabbing the boy by the scruff of his neck.

"Mum is out there!" Will shouted desperately. When he realised his voice was garbled he pulled the bottom half of his gasmask up and repeated the message.

Gaffer nodded. He looked at the sky; thick dark columns of smoke were rising up to the east.

"Looks like the far end of Kemptown got it," he said. "Well beyond Queen's Park, Will."

"I need to know," Will insisted.

"So do I lad," Gaffer nodded. "You wait here, do you understand? Wait here. Don't move. I'll get dressed, tell Gran and then we'll both go looking for your mum."

Will nodded, relieved that Gaffer was coming with him.

Gaffer had put on his helmet as well as an old khaki overcoat which made him look semi-official, like he belonged with the ARP, albeit without an armband or a proper identification mark on his helmet. Most of the Wardens wore black helmets with a white 'W' painted on it and there were other functions as well. Gaffer carried his gasmask in the cardboard box his had been issued in. Will kept his mask on and wished he had brought his catapult.

The anti-aircraft batteries had ceased firing and the plane was long gone, but the air raid warning kept on wailing as the two walked down to Queen's Park Road till that road turned west, running along the bottom of Queen's Park.

The streets were oddly busy; many folk had come outside to look at the smoke boiling up over the eastern end of town.

"Fools," Gaffer snorted. "We're fools too, Will. If the Luftwaffe send over any more bombers they'll catch half the town out in the bleeding open."

Will said nothing, he felt oddly safe with this new version of Gaffer by his side. When they came to the intersection where the road met South Avenue and Freshfield Place they turned right onto Park Street. Mum was safe; she was outside the public baths with other attendants looking at the smoke.

"Dad? Will?" She was surprised to see them.

"Will was...we were worried about you," Gaffer explained.

Some people there had been on the streets on their way to work, and a few of those confirmed it had just been a single aeroplane, one man claimed to be certain it was a Dornier DO 17 which had turned tail after dropping its bombs.

Gaffer decided to take Will further down Park Street. There was a small Salvation Army Hall at the bottom of the street where the ARP had a control centre. It was busy there, men and women were running in to report for duty whilst others ran out to jump into waiting vehicles or hop on bicycles. They all turned left onto Eastern Road, somewhere along the end of which the bombs appeared to have fallen. Gaffer walked up to one of the Wardens who was keeping gathering members of the public at bay.

"What's the situation?" Gaffer asked the Warden.

The woman looked confused, uncertain as to whether Gaffer belonged to the ARP or not. She decided that the authority in Gaffer's voice indicated that she'd better answer him.

"Single bomber, it dropped nine bombs we think. Bennet Road and Prince's Terrace got hit, Whitehawk Road too. There are fires and casualties. I don't know how many."

"Thank you," Gaffer said.

Will took off his helmet so he could remove his gasmask.

"Gaffer, can we go look?" he asked hopefully.

"Will lad, right now we'd only get in the way. Besides that they'll be pulling out bodies from beneath the rubble and gathering what they can still find of those who have been shredded by shrapnel."

Gaffer suddenly looked old and weary again. "To be frank lad, I hope that you never have to see that sight."

Will nodded, trying to hide his disappointment. They walked back home in silence.

17. FRONT ROW SEATS

The air war began to increase in intensity. Air raid warnings became the order of the day. Officially an air raid warning consisted of three phases. The first one was the signal that danger was approaching and an instruction to the general population to seek cover. The second the signal that danger was imminent at which point all the essential personnel had to seek cover too. The third was the all-clear. Sometimes though, the sirens just kept on wailing without a pause and sometimes they would start again even as the all-clear sounded. It was easy to lose track of whether or not a warning was the first or second on the days the sirens seemed to work without synchronicity, each alarm following its own course.

At Ashton Street sleeping in the cellar became permanent and Mr. Hall came over to help Gaffer strengthen two already sturdy tables with additional wooden struts and screens of wire under which the mattresses and bedding were placed.

Will expressed scepticism, if a bomb were to hit the house it was like as not to burrow itself into the cellar. Though the tables looked sturdy enough he doubted they would be much use if a Jerry bomb exploded in the cellar. Mr. Hall explained that the raid on Kemptown had destroyed six houses in their entirety, but that thirty others had been very badly damaged and it was in the buildings surrounding the impact point that these sorts of improvised shelters could mean the difference between survival and death.

Most of the air raid warnings didn't concern direct attacks on Brighton. The daytime alarms would often sound at the approach of the tiny silvery specks high up in the sky denoting Luftwaffe bombers heading inland. Almost always a pattern of vapour trails would be drawn around these formations as Spitfires and Hurricanes dived in to engage the Heinkels and Dorniers as well as their protective screen of Messerschmitt fighters. These combats would sometimes pass over deeper into English airspace but if the formations were broken up quick enough the whole would suddenly disperse; bombers diving to evade pursuing RAF fighters whilst other RAF and Luftwaffe fighters turned and twisted about each other in dog fights. Some of the planes would streak down low enough for those on the ground to hear the bursts of the machine guns.

Lessons at school were interrupted ever more frequently, sometimes up to two or three times a day and staff and pupils would huddle in the trenches, straining their necks and mesmerised by the Battle of Britain taking place right over their heads. Once, after chasing a Luftwaffe formation back across the Channel, two Hurricanes came flying back close over the rooftops and playfully performed Victory-rolls right over the school. Just about everyone scrambled out of the trenches to wave at the pilots and collectively roar approval - including many teachers. By God, but Britannia didn't just rule the waves it seemed to be master of the skies too at moments like that.

Far more dangerous for Brighton were the Luftwaffe raiders which had participated in attacks on RAF bases like Shoreham and Tangmere and flew over the town in ones and twos after the raids, releasing any bombs they had left or strafing the streets before flying back over the Channel. They tended to fly in low from the north and were hard to detect meaning the advance warning was dreadfully short. They heard it was far worse in Eastbourne where planes coming in from the west weren't spotted till the very last moment when they suddenly appeared over the South Downs which towered over the edge of town.

When they were not at school Will and Jamie would be moving from one good vantage point to another in the hope of catching a good dog fight. The view from the top of Richmond Street and Sussex Terrace, near to both their homes, was a boon of course. The hike to the Dyke Road Park was worth the effort as well. Dyke Road Park was beyond their usual bounds but the playing fields of the Brighton Hove and Sussex Grammar school now held a battery of ack-ack guns and on a lucky visit Jerry planes would pass high overhead and the ack-ack guns would start stuttering and cause puffs of black smoke to appear amidst the planes.

Will and Jamie, as well as countless of other boys, were frequently informed as to the danger by *Parkies* – usually Wardens and occasionally coppers – who did their best to keep the park clear of small boys but theirs was an almost impossible task for a bout of shooting would be followed by the very danger that was warned of: A rainfall of shiny metal pieces. Shrapnel had fast become a valued collector's item which could be proudly displayed at school or used as a trading commodity with the other boys and this outweighed the risks as far as the children were concerned.

"That was a good haul," Jamie noted with satisfaction as they departed Dyke Road Park again, half-running because one of the Parkies was making a half-hearted attempt to catch up with them. He gave up when he saw the boys exit the park.

"It sure was," Will grinned. He turned over one of his new pieces of shrapnel in his hands. Thoughtfully he added, "to shoot Jerry planes out of the sky with."

Jamie understood instantly. "We could test it, not all of it of course."

"No, just a few small pieces," Will agreed. It was clear that the qualities of used shrapnel as catapult ammunition required instant investigation.

"The Racecourse?" Jamie suggested.

Will nodded, "We'll take the doormat as well."

"Shoot as we fly!" Jamie's mouth dropped open. "Will, you're a genius."

Will grinned happily, even though the thought of combining the two activities had not occurred to him yet. The boys hastened their step.

§ § § § § §

Mum asked Brenda to go to the shops. She was hesitant because there was real danger out on the streets now. Mum said an increasing number of lads had been brought in, burnt by red-hot shrapnel they tried to pick up or bruised and cut by the stuff.

"I won't go near shrapnel," Brenda promised. She knew why she had to go. Eddie had come down with the flu and Mum preferred to nurse the feverish boy herself.

"Try and find a lemon if you can, otherwise an orange will do," Mum said, pressing some coins in Brenda's outstretched hand. "It may take a while to find a greengrocer that has them."

"If I see a queue in front of a greengrocer, I'll join it." Brenda nodded. A queue in front of a shop had become an indication that there was something worthwhile in stock.

"Good girl," Mum smiled. "You're a real dear. Be careful please."

Brenda was lucky. The nearby greengrocer knew Brenda and when she explained the situation at home he called his wife who took Brenda into the storeroom at the back of the shop. It was mostly empty packaging, food shops seldom had excess wares anymore but there was half a crate of oranges tucked into a corner. The shopkeeper's wife winked at Brenda as she carefully put three oranges in a paper bag.

"I've got one lemon left, that's all," she said regretfully. "And my own boy is ill as well."

Brenda nodded her understanding.

"So I'll cut it in half, your mum and dad are decent people," the woman decided and proceeded to do just that.

Brenda smiled.

"Best you go out back into the twitten," the shopkeeper's wife said.

"Yes, thank you so much!"

"Tell your mum I said hello, please."

"I will, thank you!" Brenda headed into the small backyard and left through the gate to emerge in the twitten. Oranges were in short supply and although they had been reserved for children it would not really do for other customers to see someone emerging from the back room with a bag. People might think there was under the counter business going on, and in a way there was, for Brenda had one more orange than was allotted.

Mum was really pleased that Brenda was back so fast and with such a treasure too.

"Please go tell them I'll drop round. Your dad will be home at six, so I can probably come around eight, after tea, to have a look at their Timothy," Mum said, then added "Brenda?"

Brenda nodded, ready for the next task.

Mum gave her a grateful smile, "Why don't you go out to play for a while?"

"Play?" Brenda was confused, "I can help you."

"You help so much already," Mum said softly. She wiped an eyelid and Brenda felt uncomfortable and wonderful at the same time. Mum made up her mind, "Go have some fun, or else you'll be missing out on too much. Be careful, stay away from the ack-ack guns. Be back at six for your tea."

Brenda nodded and then headed to the greengrocer's to pass on Mum's message. When she stepped out of the shop again she felt wonderfully free. For a moment she was absolutely delighted with the unexpected escape. Then her shoulders sagged. But what to do with it? She had given Mum back the change and had no pennies for sweets. She suddenly realised that play had always involved Eddie for a good few years now and she felt kind of empty without his little hand in hers as he scampered to keep up with her.

Then she saw Will and Jamie walking on the other side of the street. Will was wearing his ridiculously large soldier's helmet. They both had catapults tucked into their pockets and were carrying a heavy doormat as they chattered with anticipatory gleams in their eyes. Brenda tutted to herself, they were clearly up to no good. Then her eyes lit up and in a momentary lapse of reason she crossed the road and ran until she was behind them.

"Hullo Duck," Jamie greeted her.

"I am not a duck," Brenda protested.

"Quack, quack," Jamie answered and she stuck her tongue out at him.

Neither of the boys seemed surprised that she continued to follow them. They had become used to her presence, she reckoned. Good. Brenda was in a strange mood; it would be nice to just be careless for a little while. Mum had told her to go out and play so she wasn't really doing anything wrong.

§ § § § § §

They headed down Freshfield Road till they got to the hill by the Brighton Racecourse. Brenda's eyes widened as she took in the broad hill slope and she understood why the boys were carrying the doormat.

Before the war started this had been a good place to fly kites but that activity had been prohibited now and it seemed that sledding down the hill on just about anything that would slide with one, or preferably more, children perched on it was the new popular pastime.

The boys made a great fuss about placing the mat just the right way on the top edge of the slope. Then they sat down on it; Jamie in front and Will behind him.

Jamie shot Brenda an impatient look, "Well, come on then."

Will indicated the last bit of visible mat behind him and Brenda joined them tentatively. She chided herself, if she had been daring enough to follow them she shouldn't give up now.

At first the mat slid slowly and the boys helped it along by pushing the ground with their feet and grabbing tufts of grass with their hands. Brenda imitated them and suddenly the mat began to gather speed of its own. Faster and faster it went and the hillslope was treacherous because what looked like a smooth bank of grass was full of bumps which caused a rocky ride. The boys hollered their pleasure and Brenda held her breath as she felt sheer exhilaration course through her.

When they got down in one piece the mat came to a sudden halt and they spilled off, rolling over the ground, all of them laughing. They ascended the hill again for another go and Brenda felt as carefree as she had ever been.

On the third run a particularly large bump sent them sprawling off the mat and rolling down the grass. The slope was steep here and Brenda turned over and over again, the world passing by in a flurry of blurred blue and green.

Then, to her disbelief, she heard the air raid warning start up. It wailed again and again to indicate some danger in the sky and Brenda was in a momentary state of panic as the world just tumbled round and round and she couldn't see the source of possible danger.

§ § § § § §

When Will slowed down sufficiently to dare a stop he sprang to his feet to scan the sky. Jamie and Brenda did likewise.

It looked like a formation of bombers had been broken up over the Channel and the aircraft were taking evasive manoeuvres as RAF fighters closed in for a kill. Then Luftwaffe fighters pounced from the cloud cover high up, streaking down to their English foes and a dogfight broke out. Some of the jumble of planes up there suddenly hurled to much lower altitudes and the children could clearly hear the machine guns at work now.

"Germany calling, Germany calling," Jamie mimicked the German radio's English language service announcer: Lord Haw Haw.

"Get those Jerries," Will shouted his encouragement to the RAF pilots overhead. They slowly turned as the bombers and fighters made their way inland towards the open countryside around Castle Hill.

A stricken Heinkel bomber trailing smoke hurled northwards in a steadily descending trajectory low overhead. Will remembered his catapult and quickly loaded it with a bit of shrapnel. Jamie was half-a-second behind him.

"FIRE!" Will shouted and the shrapnel took to the air once more, ineffectively falling far short of the bomber. That didn't bother Will and Jamie one bit, they got off two more shots before the stricken aircraft made a getaway.

Will readjusted his helmet which was sliding over the back of his head and grunted with satisfaction.

"Looks like we got a direct hit," he told Jamie who nodded his agreement.

"Flamerinos boys!" Jamie shouted after the German plane.

"Sizzle, sizzle wonk!" Will added enthusiastically.

"What are you two on about then?" Brenda asked.

Jamie sighed and rolled his eyes at Brenda's question and Will understood. Girls. Even ones that seemed okay like Brenda never seemed to know what really mattered.

Will looked at her curiously. He didn't know why Brenda had chosen to tag along but he hadn't minded. Her little brother Eddie was always fun to have around as he instinctively understood their games. Brenda had always seemed a bit standoffish, never really joining their play though she hadn't seemed to mind watching. Will accepted her mostly because he felt her basin hair cut created a certain kinship. Today she had even been fun to have around. A lot of the girls had joined in some of the more rough and tumble games, emboldened perhaps by the sight of women driving buses and ambulances or wearing the Warden's black helmet and giving orders and instructions to both men and women. It was like having a sister he supposed and he gave Brenda a smile.

"It's all clever stuff, no rubbish!" Jamie quoted Max Miller. "They don't make 'em like Edward 'Mick' Mannock anymore, Duck!"

"I am not a duck," Brenda insisted firmly. "And I still don't know what you're on about."

"He was the best English ace in the Great War," Will explained. "Seventy three kills and a V.C. decoration. Born and bred in Brighton."

They were distracted by loud cheering and looked the other way towards the coast. A fighter had copped it in a dog fight high over the sea and was spiralling downwards tracing smoke and clearly out of control. The spectators on the hill cheered loudly; even though the plane was at such a distance that there was no way they could tell if it was British or German. As it was inconceivable that the RAF could lose a fight they automatically assumed such casualties to be German.

§ § § § § §

Brenda opened the front door. Dad turned around in the hallway. He had just got back from work and was still wearing a dirty boiler suit.

Dad looked her up and down curiously and when Brenda followed his gaze she noted with horror that her thick stockings and dress were thoroughly stained with dirt and grass. Her mouth fell open and she looked at Dad helplessly. Clothing was rationed these days and children were forever being cautioned about being mindful about this.

"Florrie?" Dad called out towards the kitchen. "Did you send Brenda out on an errand?"

"She was a real dear again earlier today," Mum's voice called back. "I told her to go out and play for a change, have some time for herself."

Dad looked back at Brenda and softly said, "It certainly looks like you did."

Brenda nodded nervously, awaiting the reaction she knew was going to come. How cross would he be?

"Charlie," Mum called out. "I need to go to the Bensons later, their lad is ill as well and they were very helpful today."

"Very well, I'll mind Edward," Dad called back and then looked at Brenda again. To her surprise he winked and then said in a low voice, "Upstairs, change into your other dress before she sees you."

Brenda smiled with relief.

"After that, you've got some washing to do," he added more sternly. "Take more care next time."

Brenda nodded and rushed up the stairs feeling like she had just crawled through the eye of a needle.

§ § § § § §

The boys were in high spirits when they got back to Sussex Street. Will had been invited for the evening meal by Jamie's dad. Mrs. Hall was visiting her sister in Lewes and Mr. Hall had decided to treat the lads to fish and chips.

Mr. Hall greeted them with a clip around the ear each on account of their shorts being exceedingly filthy, something Will and Jamie hadn't noticed yet. Only now did Will see that he had scraped his left knee and Jamie's shorts were torn by one of the legs. Other than that it did look as if they had brought half the hillside home, earth and grass had left a mark. Mr. Hall then gave them money to go to the chippie and told them to hurry before it ran out of fish.

Jamie and Will walked up Queen's Park Road. Jamie was muttering about his smarting ear but Will felt rather pleased with the light sting he still felt. For a moment it had been like having a father.

There was almost no advance warning of the approach of the Messerschmitt which suddenly appeared behind them, flying parallel with Queen's Park Road. Will and Jamie turned around as they heard the loud engine of the plane roaring at them.

"Listen to that Daimler-Benz go!" Jamie had to almost shout his admiration to be heard. "More than a 1000 HP!"

"I think it's a new 109F!" Will responded in kind.

"You DAFT LITTLE BUGGERS!" A harsh voice violated their ears as a Warden appeared out of nowhere and took a rough hold of their arms, dragging them off the street and almost throwing them into an open shop door before diving in himself.

Will scrambled up to hear the Warden cursing him for being a bloody fool. Outside there were short whistling sounds and then bangs as the Messerschmitt's pilot shot his cannons before rumbling past seemingly just a few feet over the rooftops.

Jamie got to his feet as well and both lads received their second clip around their ear that day, this time from the Warden. He kept his sermon short.

"You BLOODY well find COVER when Jerry comes."

Will and Jamie mumbled a thanks and scurried back out onto the street.

"I really think it was a 109E Will," Jamie continued the debate but stopped when they saw shiny objects on the street.

They made a quick division of labour. Jamie would go on to the chippie with the bob and sixpence his father had given him for three pieces of fish and three portions of chips. Will stayed to collect as many solid brass 20mm shells as he could. He managed to get his hand on a total of nine of them, competing with other children who came running out of shops and houses and then making a quick get-away when a Police Constable cycled up the street blowing a whistle at the children.

Will waited for Jamie at the corner of Sussex Street and they divided the spoils back at the house, giving three of the shells to Mr. Hall who was slightly shocked to hear they had been fired at but pleased with his share of the bounty none-the-less.

18. STRAFED ON ST JAMES STREET

Eddie got well again but developed the urge to visit the toilet more frequently in the evenings and Brenda would walk him to the outhouse at the back of the yard. Although the walls surrounding the little yards behind the terraced houses obscured a wider vision the night sky was often spectacular. The searchlights of the 70th Sussex Searchlight Regiment would be sweeping the sky over Brighton's seafront close by and further off they could see the beams at Worthing to the west and Ovingdean to the east. Sometimes the ack-ack guns would be spitting their anger at Luftwaffe bombers far overhead and once Brenda saw the tiny flashes of machine guns as British fighters intercepted them.

§ § § § § §

There had been talk of evacuation again. Mum and Dad were increasingly coming around to the idea that Brenda and Eddie would be much safer in the countryside. Brenda overheard the talk in the evening while she was doing her homework and she had to restrain herself from interrupting the conversation. She strongly disagreed with the notion of evacuation. Brenda couldn't even begin to imagine what it would be like to be sent away from home to live with strangers. She didn't want to leave Brighton. That night she knelt at the edge of her bed and prayed that her parents would give up on the horrible idea.

§ § § § § §

St James Street was busy with people doing their Saturday shopping. Mum had got her shopping done and led Brenda and Eddie to the sweet shop opposite St Mary's Church. She had promised them some sweets.

Eddie was wearing his cowboy outfit and Brenda had brought Margaret Elizabeth out for the walk. She usually left the doll at home, feeling a little bit too old to be seen with one on the street but poor Margaret Elizabeth had been pining for some fresh air.

The air raid warning went off as they approached the sweet shop but even before it had reached its first peak there was an ominous rumble. Brenda could see along the whole length of St James Street here, all the way to the Steine Gardens and it was there that a Messerschmitt had appeared and was now coming up from the bottom of the street, flickering lights on its wings showing that it was strafing the street .

Mum pulled Brenda and Edward into the shop hurriedly. Once inside she let go of their hands.

"Hat!" Eddie suddenly shouted and ran out again.

"EDWARD! NO!" Mum looked horrified and seemed frozen to the spot.

"Hold her," Brenda shoved Margaret Elizabeth into Mum's hand and dashed outside.

She saw the hat lying on the pavement outside, Eddie must have dropped it when her mother pulled him into the shop. Brenda ran after Eddie. In the handful of seconds since they had run into the shop and out again the Messerschmitt had come much closer, engine thundering and blazing guns barking harshly.

Brenda tackled Eddie rather roughly, throwing him onto the pavement and then diving down too to land by his exposed side. She grabbed hold of her brother and pressed him down as close to the rough surface as she could, nearly wetting herself as she heard the sequence of thuds which told her the impact trail of the machine gun bullets was sweeping straight at them.

Her back was to the plane, all Brenda could do was tilt her head towards the church. She looked straight at the now tattered gull feathers on Eddie's hat some five feet away and then there were loud cracks and fountains of grit and dust as the machine gun bullets impacted a line that passed right in between her head and the hat. Brenda could actually see the bullets bouncing off the pavement and then heard them ricocheting off the walls of nearby buildings.

The pilot of the Messerschmitt increased his altitude and then was gone altogether, leaving behind an odd silence.

Brenda scrambled to her feet and then helped Eddie up.

"You hurt me!" Eddie was astonished.

Brenda laughed much too loud. She turned to look at Mum who was still frozen in the doorway of the shop. Then mum dropped Margaret Elizabeth and rushed towards Eddie to scoop her son in her arms.

Brenda's lip began to tremble, she had heard a distinct crack. She made her way to Margaret Elizabeth and when she picked up her doll she saw that a long ugly rent ran diagonally on Margaret Elizabeth's face, there was also a chip off her nose. Brenda stared at her doll in disbelief and then looked at Mum.

"Brenda hurt me," Eddie said with a long face. Of the whole strafing attack that had made the biggest impression on him.

"That was because you were a very silly boy," Mum tried to sound stern but relief was still evident in her voice. She had seen the bullets strike the pavement mere feet from her children's heads. "You should never leave cover under fire, Edward, Never!"

Eddie lowered his head. He said softly, "Never, ever."

Mum looked at Brenda, shaking her head in disbelief. "Brenda, that was...that was..."

Brenda looked at Margaret Elizabeth's disfigured face and began to cry.

19. GÖRING SENDS HIS REGARDS

Both Gaffer and Gran were of a mind that Will would be much safer in the countryside. He wouldn't have to take the gamble of random placement of the national programmes. Will's great-uncle, Fred Maskall, worked a farm in the Weald and letters had already been exchanged so they knew Will would be welcomed there. Mum was dead set against it though. She expected the Jerries to invade any day now and would rather be close to her son when that happened. If the Jerries got a foothold they would no doubt sweep further inland towards London in which case Fred Maskall's farm offered as much safety as Brighton did. Will had no intention of leaving Brighton either, everything he knew was here and a farm in the countryside held little appeal to him. The matter had been left unsettled.

Will and Jamie met up early the next morning to head to Dyke Road Park in the hope of seeing the ack-ack guns in action. They had more than half of a bag of bull's eyes left so were adequately provisioned with sweets. The action started as soon as they reached Dyke Road Park for a damaged Heinkel 111 was struggling seawards over Hove at 2,000 feet. It was escorted by two Messerschmitt 109s but the Spitfires which appeared ignored the fighters and converged on the Heinkel. Will and Jamie began to cheer but choked back the sound when the Spitfires collided and suddenly fell away leaving a trail of wing parts in their wake. The Heinkel made its escape and Will and Jamie watched appalled as the damaged Spitfires plummeted downwards like bricks towards the rooftops of Portslade, west of Hove. It all happened in a matter of seconds and there was no time for the pilots to make an escape from the stricken aircraft.

Suddenly viewing the air war from front row seats at Dyke Road Park lost its appeal and in unspoken agreement the boys departed, wandering rather aimlessly down the Dyke Road towards the sea front. They were wary for the air raid warnings seemed to be sounding continuously and there was a lot of activity in the air as planes crossed and re-crossed the coastline, far more than had already become usual. Becoming curious again the boys agreed to go to St Nicholas Church for it was placed on a hilltop which would give them a wide view over the town.

They were just about to turn into Church Street when the sound of a low flying aircraft just overhead caused them to spin around. The boys recognised the airplane straight away; the stub beetle eyed glass nose of the Junkers Ju 88 twin engine bomber was unmistakable and the plane was close enough to discern the pilot's head behind the glass of the cockpit dome. His expression they could imagine for the aircraft was trailing smoke and both engines were coughing and spitting.

The crippled plane made a sudden dive just as it passed Will and Jamie and then struck a lamp post before hurling itself into the wall that bound the churchyard about forty feet away. Will threw himself to the ground as did Jamie. Will expected the almighty bang that followed but what struck him most were the ear-shattering screams of metal being sheared apart almost as if the airplane was a living creature that was rent asunder. He felt a warm blast of air pass over him as the shattered plane exploded into flame, filling his vision with a fiery yellow sheet and then incongruously vivid green lights as the plane's flares ignited one after the other. The roar of the fire was added to by multiple sequels of sharp cracks as ammunition ignited and Will kept his head low. Something small and black skidded to a halt right beside Will and he touched it to establish if it was burning hot. It was just warm and he absentmindedly stuck it into his pocket.

When the worst seemed to be over he scrambled to his feet, dazed by the violence of the moment which had banished the clear bright summer's day and replaced it with a dark smoky haze. Slowly he and Jamie walked forwards. The street was littered with debris, including one of the landing wheels. The engine had come to a stop against the broken churchyard wall and they could see that the tail section of the plane and parts of the fuselage had fallen beyond amidst the tombstones in the cemetery where many headstones had been knocked over and broken. Many parts of the wreck were burning fiercely.

Will stared wide-eyed at a tree on the opposite side of the road. It's branches were now garnished with torn remnants of a parachute amidst which swung the body of the Jerry pilot in a German flight suit, jagged slivers of metal protruding from his bleeding chest just below his Iron Cross and sightless eyes staring at his burning aircraft.

The boys ducked again as new rounds of ammunition started to pop off. Firemen and ARP personnel now rushed down the street. The firemen didn't hesitate when they heard the exploding ammunition and came dangerously close to the burning wreckage to extinguish it. One of the Wardens took a gentle hold of the boys and led them back down Church Street.

"Far too dangerous lads," she said kindly. "Ammo going off and the bloody thing might still have been carrying bombs."

Will and Jamie were too dazed to protest and let themselves be led away along Dyke Road and then directed towards North Street. They walked silently, still overwhelmed and occasionally looking behind them at the smoke billowing up from St Nicholas Church. Will was haunted by the sight of the dead Luftwaffe pilot; he had never seen a corpse before. Let alone a dead German enemy. It was very different from the glorious daydreams he had of using his catapult to take pot shots at Wehrmacht troopers who dared to invade his beach.

Jamie was subdued too and for a long time they were quiet. When they reached the Steine Gardens they both turned left towards the seafront. They wandered past the inaccessible entrances of the Palace Pier and the Aquarium till they had followed the Marine Parade to the characteristic seafront verandas of the Royal Crescent Mansions with their curved metal roofs and cast iron railings. There they heard the rumble of approaching aircraft again.

Suddenly an insect like Dornier Do 17 bomber thundered seawards over their heads, its bulbous head at odds with the rest of its sleek figure that ended in fragile looking twin tail fins. Two RAF fighters pursued it, Will recognised the hump-backed silhouette of Hawker Hurricanes and for a moment the dead German pilot was forgotten as both he and Jamie shook their fists at the Dornier and cheered on the Hurricanes.

The Dornier made its escape when four Messerschmitt Bf110 three seat strategic fighters streaked in from the Channel to intercept the English planes at top speed. Even though they outnumbered the Hurricanes neither the boys nor the Hurricane pilots seemed worried for the Bf110s were no match for Hurricanes or Spitfires in a dog fight. The RAF pilots dodged and evaded the incoming fire from the Bf110s and then skilfully forced two of their opponents into making turns where their slow and wide turning circles made them vulnerable to the well-judged bursts of machine gun fire from the Hurricanes.

It was over in moments, one of the Bf110's splashed into the sea, the three others high-tailed it back to France behind the now distant Dornier, one of them trailing smoke. However, one of the Hurricanes had been hit by a parting burst of German fire. Instead of following its partner into an ascent it headed straight back to the coast, its engine spluttering and the plane dropping in altitude as it approached.

To Will's surprise the defence batteries opened fire on it.

"NOOOO!" Will and Jamie shouted desperately as they saw the Hurricane shudder under the impact of incoming fire.

The plane followed an erratic course over the seafront buildings to the east, trailing smoke now and Will and Jamie ran to follow it inland even though there was no way they could keep up with it. They could still hear the thud of the impact though and arrived at the end of College Place to find a smashed rooftop of a house from which the tail section of the Hurricane protruded.

A solitary Warden stood in front of the house, visibly shaken.

"Saw it happen," he told the boys unasked. "He was trying to get to the college playing grounds to avoid the houses. Didn't make it."

Will and Jamie stared at the battered roof and tail of the plane. The Nazis seemed to have been really pressing home the attack this day. So far RAF losses had been tallied in the papers where they were just numbers which were generally cause for satisfaction because the Luftwaffe numbers were almost always higher. Today those tallies had been translated into...something different. It was a sober realisation.

They sat down on the pavement staring at the Hurricane's tail. Will sighed and put his hands into his pockets where he encountered an unfamiliar object. He recalled picking something up at St Nicholas and he took it out of his pocket. It was a very simple leather wallet without inner pockets, a little bit like a book cover really and fine workmanship too.

"Whatcha got?" Jamie was curious.

"I dunno, picked it up at St Nicholas. After the crash."

He opened it and saw a small photograph and a banknote.

"BLOODY HELL!" Jamie's eyes grew wide and he grinned from ear to ear.

Will took a closer look, ignoring the banknote for it was the photograph which intrigued him. It was a small portrait photo with white edges, the subject was a beautiful young woman. She reminded Will of that actress Nova Pilbeam he had seen in a Hitchcock picture on account of her large round eyes and dainty lips which combined to give her a smouldering look that made his heart beat faster. He turned it around to look at words penned down in elegant handwriting.

Felix. Komm bald wieder und sei vorsichtig! Ich liebe dich. B.

"It's German!" Will exclaimed.

"It bleeding well is, look at that money!" Jamie was over the moon. "Must have been that pilot's."

Will picked up the banknote to examine it.

The language was strange and the letters printed in some sort of gothic style. There was a 20 in the left corner, and a picture of a woman holding a flower in front of mountain tops on the right side of the note. Will stared at the lettering: *Reichsbanknote. Zwanzig Reichsmark.* There was a grey swastika behind the smaller lettering and an eagle astride a swastika below it.

"Can I see?" Jamie was nearly jumping up and down.

Will held up both his hands; the picture in one and the banknote in the other.

Jamie took the banknote and Will was relieved. He looked back at the handwriting on the back of the photograph. So the pilot had been called Felix. And he had a sweetheart. Will turned the photograph over and lost himself in those big brown eyes. Then he carefully put the photograph back in the wallet and closed it.

"Hang on, don't forget the banknote," Jamie said.

Will looked at him with a smile.

"Keep it Jamie, it's yours."

Jamie's mouth fell open.

"You sure?" He asked wide-eyed.

Will nodded happily. He had no idea what 20 Reichsmarks were worth, it sounded like a lot, but he doubted he would be able to buy sweets with it in Brighton. It felt good giving it to Jamie who was clearly taken with it. They agreed this material was top-secret to be hidden from all but Mr. Hall and Gaffer and then headed home.

20. LONDON IS BURNING

Gaffer had abandoned his position on the cellar stairs, insisting that Will too remain beneath the makeshift shelter of the strengthened tables. Late on Sunday night the air raid warnings had started their ominous wailing once again and it soon became clear this wasn't a clash between night fighters attacking or defending a formation of bombers headed for other targets in England. This time Brighton faced a full aerial attack.

The night's assault on the town wasn't carried out by large formations of bombers but throughout the night they could hear the heavy rumbling of bomber engines followed by the whistle and crump of bombs being released, sometimes far off and at other times close enough to feel the cellar tremble on impact. A new unknown sound was added which puzzled the cellar's inhabitants, that of thuds as if solid steel bars were being dropped on the rooftops and streets.

Gaffer took Will outside onto Ashton Street during a lull between the air raid warnings and they were greeted by the spectacle of hundreds of small bright fires coloured red, green, blue, yellow or orange.

"Incendiary bombs," Gaffer growled.

They could see ARP people around some of the closer incendiaries trying to extinguish them. Occasionally one would suddenly erupt into a small fireball as it exploded and Gaffer told Will that some of the incendiaries would have been packed with explosives and delayed trigger mechanisms as well. Will looked at the ARP workers with renewed respect for surely they must have been aware of the dangers of being obliterated by one of the explosive varieties. Fires large and small could be seen throughout the town where the incendiary bombs had set rooftops alight though some of the larger fires could also be the result of the high-explosive bombs which had been dropped as well.

"Draw out people first, with the fire bombs, then drop the heavies," Gaffer grunted with disgust. "One thing to do it on the battlefield, another to do it in a town filled with civilians. Damn Nazis."

The air raid warning sounded once again and Gaffer herded Will back into the cellar.

§ § § § § §

Will and Jamie passed a street where one of the high-explosive bombs had struck on their way to school. The sudden gap in a row of terraced houses was a surreal sight. Two houses were gone in their entirety whilst the houses to either side were badly damaged and seemed uninhabitable. One had its front wall blown away though oddly enough the now exposed interior of the house was unaffected, the table near the former wall still held a glass vase with a flower in it.

There wasn't a house left in the street with intact windows and tens of thousands of shards of glass crunched beneath their feet as they walked along the street. Firemen were just clearing up their gear and an ARP Warden encouraged Will and Jamie to keep walking, there were many of them there cordoning off the area around the damaged and missing houses.

§ § § § § §

Will, Gaffer, Mr. Hall and Jamie had walked up to the top of Richmond Street as had others from the immediate surroundings. It was the beginning of September and the evening of Black Saturday. After the incendiary bombings there had been a lull in Luftwaffe activities in Brighton with far less air raid warning interruptions than they had got used to. This evening however, it became clear that the Nazis had not yet given up the hope of a victory in the air. Late in the afternoon it had seemed as if it had been business as usual again, with high flying formations of bombers drawing the attention of RAF fighters but as it had become evening there seemed to be no end to it as wave after wave of bombers crossed the Sussex coast heading north, or left English airspace again to return to their French bases.

The BBC had reported that hundreds of bombers had attacked London's East End. Civil defence services fought the fires that were spreading. But those first attacks had taken place in the late afternoon and now, more than six hours later, waves of bombers were still crossing the coast line and heading for London. The rumour repeated atop Richmond Street was that even Brighton had been requested to send fire fighters to the beleaguered capital. This was cause for pride but then worry; as it became dark there were gasps and curses and prayers all around Will. A good deal of the northern horizon remained light, eerily orange and though it was hard to believe there could only be one explanation for that glow which even now was guiding another formation of German bombers to their target.

London was burning.

"God help those poor souls in London tonight," Gaffer said loudly.

"Amen," Mr. Hall replied.

21. SWEETS, SWEETS EVERYWHERE

Will looked outside the classroom window to see if he could spot vapour trails in the bright blue sky. It was harder than usual to focus on the lesson that was being taught; even the teachers seemed on edge these days. A certain fatigue had set in, mainly caused by the incessant air raid warnings which never did allow for a distinction between the continued aerial brawling between RAF and Luftwaffe fighters and the advent of immediate and present danger in the form of Heinkels, Junkers or Dorniers coming in on an approach run. Ever since the Luftwaffe had switched its focus to civilian targets coastal towns like Brighton seemed to have become the most logical place for returning bombers to release left-over bombs on their way back to France and there had been a marked increase in sporadic episodes of death and destruction across town. Tales of miraculous escapes or tragic deaths were told again and again. Added to this were stories of the hellish conditions in London which was being hit night after night as well as increased invasion fears. Folk had become nervous and jittery although everybody persisted in carrying on their daily business as usual, for the determination not to be intimidated by the Nazis only increased.

The sound of a low flying aircraft received instant collective focus in the classroom. There had been no air raid warning but just about everybody had learned the fallacy of relying on the wailing sirens. Will's mouth dropped open as he saw a Junkers Ju88 which appeared to be flying straight towards the school and his eyes widened when he saw the bomb bay doors swing open. Mr. Hutchinson saw it too.

"DOWN!" Under your desks now, hands behind your necks! Down!" He hollered.

Will realised there was no time to run to the trenches outside and dived underneath his desk. He could have used his bloody helmet now, he thought, but he hadn't been allowed to wear it at school for some unfathomable reason. He caught Jamie's eye and the two boys grinned reassurance at each other.

They heard the bomber roar over and for what seemed like an eternity nothing seemed to happen as the class awaited the next turn of events in complete silence. Then they heard a loud thud on the other side of school and that was followed by a deafening explosion which was quickly followed by more. The floor trembled, the windows rattled in their panes and the building seemed to shake. Then a large piece of masonry came crashing through the classroom's skylight and shards of glass fell everywhere. Some of the children screamed at that but nobody was seriously hurt.

Soon after the order sounded to assemble and to Will's surprise the teaching staff directed them to the street outside the school rather than the playground area in the back. Flanked by an ARP Deputy Chief Warden the Headmaster explained that the initial thud they had heard was a bomb that had failed to explode and now lay on the playground.

Will sucked in his breath as he realised the implication of an unexploded bomb right next to the school and sure enough the Headmaster told them they were all being sent home for the remainder of the day.

Will and Jamie had a big grin on their faces as they stepped into the day's unexpected freedom. They tried to follow the route the stick of bombs had taken and managed to get some way because thick clouds of smoke obscured them from the sight of fire fighters and ARP personnel who came rushing into the area. Glass crunched below their feet and there was rubble everywhere, as well as drifting scraps of paper and ashes. Jamie spotted a bomb fragment and tried to pick it up but let go immediately.

"Too bleeding hot," he told Will regretfully.

Will's heart stopped when they saw an arm and leg protruding from what was left of a shop front but Jamie laughed at him and told him they were parts of the mannequins which had been in the display windows. Not much further though they encountered a man covered in blood sitting on the pavement and groaning while he was being attended to by two friends.

Things became more grim when they saw a dazed survivor stumble out of the smoke bleeding profusely from a head wound after which two ARP staff ran by bearing a stretcher. The woman on it had terrible gashes on her face and an arm which was barely recognisable because fist sized chunks of flesh had been torn out of it.

Jamie grabbed Will and pulled him into a twitten.

"Let's leave here," he suggested and Will agreed. He was relieved for the sight of the wounded woman on the stretcher had shocked him and he recalled what his Gaffer had told him about the sort of sights he could expect to see immediately after a bomb had struck.

They walked to a parallel street where there was no smoke and their interest was immediately focused on groups of children running down the street in a state of excitement.

"What's going on?" Jamie shouted at one of the boys who was in their class.

"Parsons Confectionary got it Jamie." The boy didn't stop but shouted an answer. "Sweets all over the place, the whole ruddy street filled with sweets!"

Will and Jamie started running immediately. They turned left at the bottom of the street. The actual building was still standing. The last bomb had fallen in the courtyard behind Parsons Confectionary but the force of the blast had blown most of the content of the ground floor right out onto the street. All of the glass jars seemed to have been shattered and tens of thousands of glass fragments reflected the sunlight thus enhancing the bright colours of the sweets which were truly everywhere just as if the road had been paved with them. Dozens of children were already scrabbling for the sweets, some of them with bleeding hands where the glass had cut them but that didn't stop them. Jamie dashed straight in but Will came to a halt.

"Oh!" was all he could say. This was the sort of thing he daydreamed about sometimes, a town made of sweets like that house in the fairy tale.

Then he saw Mrs. Parsons sitting on the kerb opposite her shop.

He knew she had managed to keep the store running after her husband's death and was always kind. She was one of the few who would sometimes sell ha'penny worth of sweets to the less-well off kids in the area.

Some of the same kids who were now scrambling around laughing excitedly as they tried to sweep up as many free sweets as they could.

"Hullo, Will," a voice suddenly said next to Will. Will glanced sideways and saw Brenda clutching a doll with a cracked face.

"Oh hullo Brenda," he replied absentmindedly. He looked at Mrs. Parsons again. She seemed to be totally oblivious to the looting of her inventory; she just sat on the kerb and was quietly crying as she took in the devastated interior of her store.

"You feel sorry for Mrs. Parsons too?" Brenda asked shyly.

Will nodded; there was something about the sight of the tearful woman surveying the wreckage of the business her deceased husband had built up that touched him. It did look dreadful in there. The blast had even ripped up the floorboards and deposited these in front of the shop like an uneven pack of shuffled cards.

Will and Brenda crossed the street too, carefully so because of all the debris on the street. Will saw that Mrs. Parsons was hurt some, mostly light cuts caused by flying glass he figured. He came to a stop in front of her but she didn't seem to notice him; just sat there with her hands on her lap, gently rocking as tears flowed down her cheeks. Will didn't know what to do or say. What do you say to someone when they are looking at the destruction of their livelihood? The torn remnants of precious memories?

Brenda led the way; she sat down next to Mrs. Parsons without a word and took one of the old woman's hands into her own. Brenda gave Will an impatient nod and he followed suit, sitting down on Mrs. Parsons' other side and taking her other hand into his. He felt vaguely embarrassed at first and hoped the other lads wouldn't see. When he saw that they were far too busy scooping up their booty to even notice anything else he suddenly couldn't care less about their opinion.

They sat there for a long time, the boy, girl and shopkeeper; for the ARP and other emergency services had their hands full with the seven explosions which had rocked the streets behind Parsons Confectionary.

The helmets showed the variety of personnel involved. A man with a white helmet with a black 'W' on it – Will knew this was a District Warden – directed the other Wardens in forming a cordon around the entry to the street which led to the places where the bombs had impacted. The rescue 'R' and ambulance 'A' helmeted workers were the ones moving up that street just as the fire fighters were. There were a number of police constables as well and a few lucky older kids who carried the white 'M' on their black helmets and arrived on their bicycles. These were the messengers who would convey messages between a site like this and whatever local ARP post was co-ordinating the response. Will had applied to become a messenger but had been told he was too young and ownership of a bicycle was a prerequisite too.

Neither of the children spoke till at last a concerned Warden approached the three and motioned some of her colleagues over.

"Let's get you to a shelter dear," she told Mrs. Parsons. "A nice hot cup of tea will do you good. With some extra sugar for the shock."

"Thank you children," Mrs. Parsons said softly as she was helped up.

Brenda looked at Will inquiringly after Mrs. Parsons had been led away. Will felt his eyes water and cursed himself for being soft. Without a word he turned and ran away.

22. THE GHOST COMES HOME

Though many might have despaired in private moments Brightonians made a point of carrying on. To give up was to accept defeat at the hands of the Nazis. These had shown their true face now. Strafing children on busy streets and parcelling out death and destruction willy-nilly were not tactics to be honoured by lowering the head in submission. If the Jerries wanted a surrender they had better sail over and jolly well walk up the beaches and ask for it in person. Even then they would find this a tedious business. The Dutch, Belgian and French citizens hadn't been prepared, people told each other. Their loss had been Britain's gain for all now knew what treatment they could expect if there was an invasion. There was a grim stubborn determination to show the Germans what it meant when folk said "Sussex wun't be druv." Even an old war veteran in long johns armed with a shotgun and a small boy in pyjamas armed with a catapult might be able to take out at least one well trained parachutist between them.

Will just hoped that the parachutist wouldn't be carrying a picture of a German sweetheart on him. Like the one that had belonged to Felix, the dead Luftwaffe pilot he had seen hanging in the tree at St Nicholas Church. It had started to worry him.

Komm bald wieder und sei vorsichtig! Ich liebe dich.

Gaffer had translated it for him. *Come back soon, be careful. I love you.*

It was probably a sign that the chap wasn't quite like all the other Jerry thugs, Will had decided. Nobody could write a message like that to a monster. That brought a new worry.

He decided to ask Gaffer about it. Indirectly of course, Gaffer mustn't start to doubt Will's patriotism.

"Gaffer?"

Gaffer looked up from the paper he was reading. "Will, my lad?"

"In the war, the Great War...," Will paused. Gaffer nodded for him to continue. "The Huns who were shelling you, did you think they were...all evil?"

Gaffer seemed to understand what he was asking. "Most of them were just doing their job, Will. The prisoners I saw sometimes, being led to the rear, they seemed like ordinary blokes to me."

"But they were trying to kill you," Will pointed out.

"Refusing to obey an order warranted the death penalty, Will," Gaffer said slowly. "You would be shot."

"The Huns did that?"

"The English did too," Gaffer said quietly. Then he turned back to the newspaper. He didn't like to talk about the Great War.

Will was speechless anyway. He could not believe the British had executed their own soldiers. They were the good side, weren't they? Gaffer wouldn't lie though.

Komm bald wieder und sei vorsichtig! Ich liebe dich.

War was clearly more complicated than Will had anticipated.

§ § § § § §

For the Terrible Trio carrying on as normal meant going to the pictures. Mr. Hall treated the lads to *Dark Command* in August. They all liked westerns and to see John Wayne and Roy Rogers play in the same movie was a treat. Will also liked the Civil War setting, he had a crazy longing to one day own a US cavalry man outfit, the neat yellow stripe down the sides of the light blue trousers and a dusty dark blue military coat would suit him, he reckoned. He saw himself charging down the racetrack hill on horseback waving a sabre and holding a lance with a white and red striped pennant streaming from it while hapless Wehrmacht soldiers fled in panic in front of him. All of them conveniently without *Ich liebe dich* pictures.

At the beginning of September they had gone to see Errol Flynn in *The Sea Hawk* and that was even better. Swashbucklers were good to begin with of course, especially if Flynn played in them, but the setting of an England threatened with invasion by the Spanish Armada was superb and Will rooted for the English privateer most fervently.

In Mid-September Mr. Hall proposed going to see the comic drama *The Ghost Comes Home*, declaring that they could all use a laugh. Will and Jamie fully agreed.

§ § § § § §

"Mum?" Brenda walked out of the kitchen and into their small yard.

"Lend us a hand, please dear," Mum was doing laundry. She was boiling one wash but another was ready for the wringer.

"Mummy!" Eddie called from the kitchen doorway.

Brenda hurried to him, ushered him into the kitchen and shut the door. Eddie wasn't allowed in the yard when a wash was boiled.

Then she helped her mother. Washing was a physically hard chore in all its stages and before too long they were both perspiring.

"It's a good thing ladies don't sweat, isn't it Mum?" Brenda asked cheerfully. "Otherwise I'd feel a bit icky."

"Icky?" Mum raised an eyebrow. "Since when did you start speaking American?"

"I heard it at the pictures," Brenda said. "I wrote it down in my Interesting Word Notebook."

"You and your notebooks," Mum shook her head.

"There's a matinee, this afternoon," Brenda said carefully. "Some friends asked if I wanted to come along."

She had been elated at school when a couple of the girls had asked her to come. She wasn't asked often and hoped fervently that Mum wouldn't give the answer which she dreaded.

"That's nice," Mum said. "I've got just enough change for two tickets. Edward would probably enjoy it too."

Brenda felt her hopes sink. She didn't think the girls would like it if she showed up with Eddie in tow. Or rather, that is what she told herself. Secretly, it would be nice if, just this once, she could go out on her own.

"Mum, can't I go alone?" Brenda said and then quickly added, "with my friends."

Mum looked at her, "I am working this afternoon. Till late. Your dad is on a late shift as well. Edward is your brother. Do you propose leaving him on his own? Who will make his tea?"

Brenda bowed her head.

"I am sorry, Brenda," Mum said. "But we all have to do our bit. I am disappointed in you."

"I'll take Eddie," Brenda conceded. It wouldn't be so bad. Eddie could charm just about anyone, the girls might even like him a great deal.

"No," Mum said. "It's too late for that now. You've had your chance. I want you to think this over, very carefully."

They finished the washing in silence. There was tension between them and Brenda didn't like it but neither did she think it was very fair of Mum. She hadn't thought about her parents' shifts, that was true but sometimes it seemed that she never got time to just be on her own for a while.

Later that afternoon, after Mum had left for the RSCH, Eddie came into the living room with *The House at Pooh Corner.*

"Tigger time," he announced happily. "Tigger, Tigger, Tigger!"

For a very brief moment Brenda felt anger flare up and she wanted to tell him that she didn't want to read to him today. Then she imagined his face if she told him. He wouldn't understand and then he'd be upset. It wasn't his fault.

She forced a smile and nodded. The Hundred Acre Wood awaited. Eeyore, perhaps, would understand how she felt.

§ § § § § §

Will, Jamie and Mr Hall set off for Kemptown to the matinee at the Odeon Cinema on St George's Road. People called it the 'Titchy' as there was another bigger Odeon in West Street.

None-the-less the auditorium at the Titchy was far from small, it could seat hundreds of people and about 300 – mostly children- filled the auditorium this Saturday afternoon. Mr. Hall had got good seats in the middle of the front stalls.

The show started with newsreels which told terrible tales of atrocities taking place in occupied Europe and were followed by various informative pieces. Will liked the *Food Flash* this time warning people not to throw away food.

"Bread and money are both worth dough," the man on the screen said and Will smiled.

The next person to appear on the screen was a fat chubby man who said it was generally expected that people in the pictures had S.A. and that he had a very special S.A. The adults and older children laughed, they knew that S.A. stood for Sex Appeal and this man certainly had none of that. He grew more serious and explained that he was making a Spade Appeal in the Dig for Victory campaign. They saw pictures of factory workers and school children growing crops and tending these in their breaks. Will and Jamie shared a glance; they wouldn't mind such a project at school.

Will liked the catch line too. *Straight from the plot to the pot!*

The next two items were dull. One exhorted everybody to eat more carrots but Will reckoned they already ate more than enough carrots at Ashton Street so didn't really need to be told. The second was called *Two Cooks and a Cabbage* and was an instructive film for young girls to cook properly when called to do so at home and not ruin good food by being careless. Will and Jamie yawned loudly.

They paid more attention during a longer dramatization which drove home the message *Make do and mend*. In it a moth balled suit belonging to a soldier who had gone off to war started talking to the soldier's wife when she took it out for a jaunt down memory lane. Will liked the concept of a talking suit. It would be smashing if his helmet could talk he was sure.

Then the main feature started. It was not bad, Will decided, though he thought the main character Vern just a bit too foolish. The story was interesting though but when Vern had just come home to find that his family had spent the travel insurance money paid out because he was supposed to have been lost at sea the movie was suddenly stopped.

The audience let out a collective groan as a familiar message was flashed on the screen.

An AIR RAID WARNING has just been received. The management suggest you remain in the building but anyone desiring to leave is free to do so now. The Performance will continue.

Will sighed as the lights came on. The whole magic of going to the pictures was broken by these interruptions. An alternative reality which formed a short sweet escape from the world out there shattered like a pupil's daydream was rudely obliterated by the sarcastic tongue of a teacher. Nobody left to go outside anyhow; the Luftwaffe could already be sweeping down to strafe the streets again or shrapnel and broken glass could be flying about. After a few minutes the lights were dimmed again and the movie resumed.

§ § § § § §

Around half past three in the afternoon of Saturday 14 September a Dornier bomber appeared in the sky over Brighton. It had been split off from its squadron by a Spitfire which was chasing it. In order to facilitate its escape the pilot decided to jettison its full load of bombs. Twenty 110 pound bombs rained down on Kemptown. They hit Edward Street, Upper Rock Gardens, Hereford Street, Upper Bedford Street, Rock Street and Kemp Town Place. One of the bombs headed for St George's Road and scored a direct hit on the Odeon Cinema.

§ § § § § §

Suddenly there was a loud rattling on the roof of the cinema. Will looked up and started to frown but then there was an almighty crash as parts of the ceiling came down to his right. This was followed by a tumultuous explosion which lit up the darkened auditorium like fiery lightning. Will's face felt as if had received a nasty sun-burn in a fraction of a second after which his vision went entirely red for a second.

The blast had knocked the air out of Will's lungs and for what seemed like forever he was stunned into immobility and a deafening silence. The smell was awful. When he regained his movement everything he perceived seemed to be in slow motion and Will had trouble interpreting what he saw. Smoke and dust had filled the auditorium with a murky fog. This was thickest by the right front stalls where it was incongruously penetrated by beams of sunlight which streamed through a massive jagged chasm in the ceiling.

A few figures stumbled from that hellish turmoil of dark smoke and fierce light. Children; a girl clutching the remnants of a shattered arm, a boy trailing shiny blue coils from a gaping hole in his belly. Their mouths were open; they must have been screaming but Will couldn't hear a thing. He looked sideways at Mr. Hall for reassurance and clarification but Mr. Hall no longer seemed to have a head on his shoulders so was quite incapable of giving an answer. Someone would have to fix that. Will wondered if he was deaf because of the blood, his entire head seemed to be soaked in warm liquid and he could feel it pulsing out of him somewhere on the right side of his scalp.

Everything became black and Will passed out.

23. AT THE ROYAL SUSSEX COUNTY HOSPITAL

When Will came to he was surprised to find himself outside on the street for he couldn't recall walking out. He was lying down on the pavement opposite the Odeon and admired its long rectangular white façade for a moment. The line of small square windows which ran along the entire length of the front of the building as well as the simple square gable always reminded him of a fort somewhere in south-western America. Will himself of course, would conduct the heroic defence of the fort; the windows made perfect gun embrasures and the attackers would be astonished to find Will had placed a proper cannon behind each of them.

It really did look like a siege now, he reflected with a strange sense of contentment. Men in helmets were running in and out of the front door, there was debris everywhere and foul smoke drifted from the roof. With disappointment he registered that he must have been fighting on the wrong side for the pavement around him was covered with bodies. Some screaming – he could hear them now – others shaking convulsively or crying; in loud wails or soft sobs. Some didn't move at all. There were folk shuffling around on the street as well, with torn clothes and cuts and gashes. They looked completely dazed. Will's cannon trick must have worked.

A nearby pub emptied, the customers running to the entrance of the cinema and then going in. Will frowned. The Wardens should have stopped them, you couldn't just go running in and out of bombed buildings. He had come to the conclusion that this is what must have happened. He had been bombed. He wondered where Jamie was and tried to scramble up but his body was refusing to co-operate. Suddenly a whole gaggle of white uniformed nurses came charging down the street, they were joined by the landlady of the pub who rushed to them with her arms full of tea-towels. They were followed shortly after by ambulances. It was funny, Will thought, that the nurses had outraced the ambulances. Then again the hospital was real close. That was good, wasn't it?

Some of the nurses rushed to the cinema entrance where Wardens and others –including a vicar- were emerging with bloody bundles in their arms. Other nurses –armed with tea-towels now- strode to the pavement where Will lay to start bandaging as many as they could. People came out of their houses, sometimes covered in glass and cuts themselves, with tea-towels and bed sheets which were cut into strips on the spot. A few children were being helped into private cars but then a number of buses drove up and the drivers evicted their passengers and helped the nurses load the wounded onto the bus. Will hoped they would take him as well; he had no money for the bus fare but his head was starting to smart badly now. He passed out again as they helped him into the bus.

§ § § § § §

Royal Sussex County Hospital was on Eastern Road, very close to St George's Road . The Outpatient Department on the other side of Eastern Road had been designated as the casualty clearing station and it was here that Will was brought like many other children and adults. He lay on a stretcher on the floor, far more comfortable than the pavement and considered himself lucky as those brought in later had to lie on the floor. He tried to shut his ears to the cries of pain and distress.

Medical staff walked about as fast as they could though there was little space for them to walk and yet more wounded were brought in.

A doctor came closer inspecting their injuries.

"This is no use, she's gone," he said to the ambulance men carrying the stretcher. "Straight to the mortuary please."

"Shrapnel in the leg," he peered at another. "He'll have to wait his turn, set him down in that corner."

"Immediate treatment, next door to the right if you please." The doctor was rushing from one to the next trying to create some order in the mayhem. He walked to Will.

"This little chap is fair covered in blood, we need to see what caused it, next room please," he motioned to two Wardens who had just brought in one of the walking wounded.

Will's stretcher was lifted up and he was carried down a corridor. New tumult broke out by the entrance as distraught parents and grandparents were now pushing their way in, frantic with worry and most panting as if they had come running from the Odeon as fast as they could.

He was brought into a smaller room which was already fairly full, two doctors and three nurses were attending those on stretchers. Will was set down next to a girl whose eyes rolled in her skull as she mumbled incessantly and sometimes called out for her mum. He looked down and saw that that her knee was shattered; it wasn't even recognisable as a knee, just a mass of meat with shards of bone sticking out.

Will looked to his other side. He felt sorry for the girl but she was making him feel queasy. His head hurt as he turned it but he smiled in relief when he saw the familiar face of Jamie next to him. Jamie seemed alright. His face was dirty and had some dried blood on it and his skin had a strange pallid waxy colour. His eyes were closed, he must have been asleep.

One of the nurses came to Will and started gently cleaning his head with a moist cloth. It felt nice and Will felt almost relaxed, he had found Jamie and the nurse was very beautiful and she was being ever so sweet. Although she was all serious now there was a cheeky quirkiness about her which reminded him of Googie Withers whom he had seen in several pictures at the Twitchy.

He winced.

"Does it hurt anywhere else lad?" The nurse asked.

Will nodded but the movement made him wince again.

"I think my arm..."

"There's a gash in it alright. I'll clean that with iodine in a minute, it'll sting but it looks like we can just stitch it up. It's your head I am worried about."

"You need to fix Mr. Hall."

She nodded and then called one of the doctors over. The doctor bent over for a look.

"Shrapnel in the skull, just behind his right ear. Add him to the list, that'll need an operation. Any more wounds?"

"I should have worn my helmet," Will told them.

"Just his arm. I think most of this blood isn't his own doctor."

The doctor left and the nurse tended to Will's arm.

Another nurse – who looked vaguely familiar - came in with two stretcher men; she had a blanket over her arms and started to cover Jamie up with it. The nurse who was treating Will looked at her questioningly.

"His mum is out there, in the corridor. She's a neighbour of mine. We don't want her to see him just yet when he's taken away, not in the midst of all that mayhem," the new nurse explained.

"But she'll want to see him, if it's Jamie's mum she'll be worried," Will protested.

The nurses exchanged a look.

The new nurse pulled the blanket over Jamie's face and motioned the men who lifted up the stretcher.

"No, wait," Will struggled but was held down firmly by the nurse who had been treating his arm as Jamie was carried away.

"You can't do this!" Will shouted. "Where are you taking Jamie?"

He started sobbing. The nurse had seemed so nice and now she was holding him down and they wouldn't even let Jamie and his mum see each other. What if Will's mum showed up? Would they be kept apart as well?

Will was thoroughly bewildered and when the nurse spoke soft words of comfort to him he started crying as an inconsolable sadness overwhelmed him.

§ § § § § §

The rest of the evening passed in a blur. Will remained in the same room as new wounded were brought in and others taken away. His mum was brought in; she was distraught and could only cry for the first five minutes after she came in. Later Gaffer and Gran came to visit too. The adults consulted with each other and with the hospital staff in low hushed voices. Late that night Will was rolled out of the room on a proper trolley. He saw that the corridors and waiting rooms had been cleared of the wounded, though there were many anxious relatives milling about, some being comforted by members of the clergy. Will had heard Mum say that the Bishop of Lewes had been there all afternoon and evening and he had even helped her to find Will.

The last thing Will saw before he was rolled into an operation theatre was a nurse and an ARP warden mopping up puddles of blood in the corridor. There were a lot of white-masked people in the operation theatre who all looked at him and that made him feel important as he was anaesthetised. He was mixing with Bishops and doctors now and tried to grin but was becoming strangely mellow and then swallowed up by oblivion.

§ § § § § §

The shrapnel was removed and when Will came to in a clean bed in a ward he was presented with the chunk of metal by a doctor. The man congratulated Will for having a thick skull for it had stopped the shrapnel from puncturing his brain. He would have to stay for a few weeks because they needed to be absolutely sure there was no lasting damage. The doctor left Will turning the shrapnel in his hands round and round as he frowned. The wards were all full and he and another boy lay in the corner of a woman's ward with about thirty women and girls in it. It was somehow unmanly but there wasn't much he could do about it.

Mum came round with Gaffer, both of them heavily laden. As requested they had brought Will's helmet, catapult, bag of Class-A ammunition (marbles), bag of Class-B ammunition (beach pebbles), three brass 20mm shells and a battered biscuit tin which held his best shrapnel pieces. He proudly showed them his latest addition which, having been stuck in his skull, was now obviously his favourite. They had also brought his pyjamas which was good for his shorts and shirts were torn badly. Better yet, they had bought, begged and borrowed from various neighbours and this had earned them a big paper bag filled with sweets and chocolates, more than Will had ever owned at any one time.

He peered into the bag and started happily listing the names of the sweets he saw, missing the glance Mum and Gaffer exchanged.

"There's this too," Gaffer grumbled.

Mum produced a wooden model of a Spitfire just like the one Jamie had. Will's eyes grew large, there was only one person who made them like that, they must have fixed Mr. Hall up pretty quick.

"We spoke to Mrs. Hall. She'll be moving to her sister's house in Lewes. She wanted you to have this."

Will tentatively took the Spitfire, it seemed wrong.

"Jamie will have the Hurricane to play with, I guess," he said.

"Jamie is dead Will, you must understand," Mum said.

"I know what," Will cheered up. "I'll just borrow it, till I get better. Jamie can have it back afterwards."

Mum's eyes teared up which made Will feel uncomfortable so he went back to naming his sweets.

"Pear drops! And look, at least three acid drops and a gobstopper!"

24. DUCK NO MORE

Mum came home in a total state. Her nurses uniform was covered in blood stains and she threw herself into Dad's arms and started sobbing inconsolably.

"Mum?" Brenda asked worriedly. She had heard that there had been a terrible bombing raid in Kemptown but only now realised that the SRCH would have received the wounded.

"Mummy?" Eddie's eyes were large.

"Some of them," Mum sobbed in Dad's arms, "had metal springs from the cinema seats lodged in them."

"Brenda, take Eddie upstairs," Dad ordered curtly while he stroked his wife's head.

"But..."

"Now, Brenda!" He growled and she took Eddie by the hand to lead him upstairs.

"I want mummy!" Eddie wailed.

"Mum needs to be with Dad," Brenda said, her voice bereft of emotion. She really wanted to wail too but that would send Eddie into a state for sure. "We can read from the Jungle Book, would you like that?"

"Tigger," Eddie decided and Brenda nodded.

Later she slipped downstairs into the kitchen. She made tea and some sandwiches. She brought a tray into the living room. Her parents were on the couch, Dad was sitting down on one side and Mum lay on his lap, her eyes staring blindly at the wall.

"Thank you, Brenda," Dad said, and nodded reassurance at her.

She nodded back and then went to the kitchen to fetch the other tray because Eddie needed something resembling tea.

Dad came upstairs later, after she had put Eddie in bed. Brenda was on her bed trying to read the Jungle Book but she couldn't focus on Mowgli's adventures this time.

"I didn't mean to be cross with you, sweetheart," Dad apologized. "Thank you for making tea, Mum really couldn't manage."

Dad sat on the edge of the bed and stroked Brenda's hair. She sighed. It had been a long time since he had last done that.

"It was bad?" Brenda asked carefully.

Dad nodded grimly. "It was pure hell."

"Will she be all right?" Brenda asked worriedly.

"She's asleep now, she'll feel better in the morning," Dad nodded. "Brenda, there is something I need to tell you."

Brenda nodded.

"I am afraid some neighbours were involved," Dad said.

"The Clarkes?" Brenda asked curiously. The old couple next door rarely ventured out of their house anymore.

"No, the Halls."

Brenda felt her chest go tight. *Not Jamie, please, not Jamie.*

"I am afraid that Mr. Hall and their lad were in the cinema. They both died, it was instant."

Brenda shook her head.

"Your mum saw the boy herself."

"Jamie, his name i...was Jamie," Brenda felt her eyes well up.

Jamie. Gone.

She began to cry and didn't even notice when Dad lifted her up and pressed her shaking body to him as he uttered meaningless sounds of comfort.

All she wanted to hear was a cheeky voice calling her 'Duck'.

25. DOROTHY'S LEFT LEG

That first night in the ward was uncomfortable. Will had heard the occasional suspicious noise from Mum or Gran, especially in the cellar where all of them slept close together, but he had never realised that women farted just as much as men till he spend a night in a ward with thirty of them. A couple were there for bowel problems and they were the worst. Farts were fun when you were mucking about with a bunch of mates in Queen's Park, but not coming from girls and women in a hospital ward. It somehow didn't seem right. Even worse, a couple of them really snored; the kind of deep sawing sound that made your spine tremble every time you heard it.

Will lay on his back staring unhappily at the ceiling, or at least he assumed it was the ceiling for it was entirely dark and here too thick black-out curtains had been drawn shut. The biggest problem, he slowly came to realise as he felt the pressure on his bladder, was that he had to pee. There was a chamber pot beneath his bed but he felt very nervous about getting his willy out in a room full of strange women – girls even – whether it was pitch black or not.

He held it as long as he could but in the end he had to scramble onto the floor because it would be far more embarrassing to wet his bed. He picked up the chamber pot and wormed his way behind the black-out curtain and sighed a breath of relief as he aimed his willy into the pot and peed for what seemed like ages.

When he emerged from behind the curtain – careful so as not to spill the contents of the pot- he was relieved because nobody could have possibly seen him though he was slightly worried that somebody might have heard. He listened carefully but all he heard was the continuous snoring of the snore champion on the other side of the ward and a monumental fart in the far corner which lasted for at least half a minute. That woman would have been elevated to a deity in Queen's Park, Will decided.

He decided to reward himself with a sweet and then felt guilty for not sharing his sugary treasure with Jamie. He recalled seeing Jamie in the hospital and decided to go find him. He put on his helmet in case there was a bombing raid and clutched the bag of sweets under his arm. He'd leave the Spitfire for now and ask Jamie if it was alright for him to borrow it till they got out of hospital.

One of the nurses found him drifting along a corridor peering into dark wards and gently steered him back to his bed.

§ § § § § §

Will learned to know some of the other patients in his ward. The other boy was a lad called Ken whose forearm had been mauled by shrapnel and whose face had been scratched badly too. There was a woman who had also had a piece of shrapnel embedded in her head and Will felt a special kinship with her on account of that. There was a girl his age called Dorothy who had a part of a cinema seat spring removed from the calf on her left leg and another partial spring from her thigh on the same leg. She insisted on showing him her leg and at first Will felt uncomfortable but soon they made it into a game where Will came to inspect it twice a day and assured her she was healing well, mesmerised by the light curvature of her lower thigh which became visible each time she pulled up her nightie. It somehow made sleeping in a woman's ward easier, knowing Dorothy's left leg was only two beds over at night.

§ § § § § §

St Peter's Church on London Road was filled for the memorial service for over 50 people who died in the bombing raid on September 14. Those wounded who had been allowed to leave the hospital for the service were given a place of honour at the front but Will barely registered what was said at the service, nor did he derive any pleasure from having front row seats in the magnificent gothic building which had often played a part in his imagination when he played Ivanhoe.

He had seen Mrs. Hall before the service but barely recognised her. She was dressed in black and supported by her sister, looking haggard, pale and withdrawn. Gaffer had come to the hospital two days before and taken Will for a stroll in the hospital grounds for a man-to-man talk about Mr. Hall and Jamie. Will had still had trouble accepting that the other two members of the Terrible Trio had died in the bombing of the Odeon. He was still eagerly waiting for Mr. Hall to march into the ward and announce that he had a proposal as his eyes glinted with mischief. Though he had shared the chocolate in his special treats bag with Ken and Dorothy Will only allowed himself one sweet a night, just before lights-out. He felt obliged to save the rest so he could share it with Jamie who had so often shared with him.

Mum gently guided Will to Mrs. Hall after the service was over and people stood outside shaking their heads and talking in sober tones.

"My condolences Mrs. Hall."

Will squeaked the words his Gaffer had taught him to say but he looked away in guilt, maybe she would be angry at him because Jamie and Mr. Hall were gone and he wasn't. The unfairness of that troubled Will himself as well.

Mrs. Hall broke down and swept him up in a tearful embrace. He could feel her body shaking violently and felt embarrassed but tentatively wrapped his arms around her shaking back.

"They'll have plenty of beano pies to eat now," he tried to comfort her. "And Mr. Hall will have all the time he wants to build toys."

Mrs. Hall broke down completely at that and was led away by her sister and Will felt bad for making her feel worse.

He was vaguely aware that Brenda and Eddie came towards him. Brenda to stumble through an awkward condolence. She looked pale and upset. Eddie proudly showed Will a lead farm animal he had been playing with and Will nodded dumbly.

He let Gaffer lead him to the special bus that would take him back to the Royal Sussex County Hospital. That night, after lights out, he cried himself to sleep. Quietly of course, for he didn't want Dorothy to hear.

§ § § § § §

It was past three on a Sunday and Will was looking forward to his second daily inspection of Dorothy's leg. The day before she had encouraged him to trace the skin around the scar tissue of the lower wound with his index finger and this morning had extended that invitation to include the scar tissue of the wound above her knee as well. Will was looking forward to a repetition of that treatment of her leg. Dorothy's skin had felt soft, warm and smooth under his finger and he felt sure it would be conducive to her quick recovery.

"Conducive," he repeated again. He had heard a doctor use the word and was very impressed with it. Then his face contorted as the air raid warning sounded from several quarters of town. This was soon followed by the ominous rumbling of low flying aircraft and the chorus of ack-ack and Bofors guns by the seafront. Nurses rushed in and helped those who could get out of bed to crawl underneath the beds. There was no time to evacuate the ward.

Dorothy made the most of the confusion and crawled behind the beds until she reached Will who sat crouched, pushing his helmet tightly down on his head with both hands as he trembled. Dorothy pressed herself against his side and he could feel her trembling too. Somewhere deep inside him Will wanted to man up, be brave and protective towards the girl but the cacophony of sirens, plane engines and anti-aircraft fire outside made him feel nauseous and he started shaking more violently. Ken joined them now, taking place on Dorothy's other side, and the three children huddled together, trying to make themselves as small as possible and trying to make the shivering stop by wrapping their arms tightly around each other.

One of the ward nurses looked under the bed, looking comically surprised at first at the sight of the three of them and then tried to give them a reassuring smile even though she was nervous too. Then she was distracted by the woman who had also had a shrapnel head wound and was now trying to make for the door of the ward; shouting that she didn't want to be trapped in a building again, that she needed to be outside in the open. She was restrained by several nurses who urged her to remain calm. Will understood what the woman meant though. He felt trapped too, constrained by the bed and other hospital floors over his head. Even now a bomb could be hurling itself downwards in their direction and he would have joined the woman's escape attempt except Dorothy had her arms wrapped tightly around his neck and the sense of her warm body pressed into him was something that was nice and interesting, despite his fears. It prevented him from breaking into panic altogether at any rate.

They heard the familiar whistles, far away enough but Will suddenly had a parched feeling in his throat and he could feel his heart thump manically in his chest. A whole series of crumps and subsequent explosions followed, one after the other and that was followed by the now familiar rattling of the windows and shaking of the ground.

The all-clear brought relief till about half-an-hour later when the first victims were brought into the hospital and the rumour started spreading in the wards that Albion Hill had copped it.

"I live there," Will whispered fearfully.

"So do I," Dorothy nodded.

The children refused to get out from under the bed which suddenly seemed the only thing which could protect them from the Nazi campaign of aerial terror. Though their shaking had stopped they now clutched each other for moral support as they struggled and then fought with dark fears concerning flashes of fire and billowing clouds of smoke and dust on Albion Hill.

They only let go of each other when parents at long last showed up and they scrambled from underneath the bed to hurl themselves into familiar grown-up arms.

The news was bad; bombs had landed all over Albion Hill; including Cambridge Street, Ashton Street and Sussex Street. Mum told Will that Gaffer's house was still standing but that it had not a single glass window left. Parts of the street had become rubble. Mr. Chubb the butcher had died when his butcher's shop was struck and the newsagent at number 13 had been completely obliterated.

Before Mum left one of the nurses had an urgent hushed conversation with her and as the two kept on looking in Will's direction he assumed it concerned him.

Mum came back the next day with Gaffer in tow and they sat down next to the hospital bed and told Will that they had decided he was to be evacuated.

"Evacuated?" Will whispered. Away from Brighton? He threw a glance at Dorothy. Who would take care of her left leg if Will wasn't around?

"Yes, Fred, your father's uncle, in the Weald. He'll take you in until the war is over. It's got too dangerous lad." Gaffer said.

"But you and Gran...and Mum..." Will protested feebly.

"Have livelihoods here," Gaffer answered. "You're a brave lad Will, but you've been through enough as it is. The decision is final."

Will looked at Mum for support. She swallowed visibly and then looked away. He lowered his head miserably and then nodded a meek acceptance.

26. BRENDA

The train engine started chuffing faster as the train departed from the station. Brenda's compartment was filled with children, all wearing a label around their neck and carrying not only a suitcase or bag and their gasmask, but also a packed lunch. Brenda waved at Mum and encouraged Eddie to do the same. When the platform was out of sight she sat down and looked around her inquisitively.

Some of the children around her were chattering happily, quite excited by the whole adventure. Others were teary-eyed and frightened. Then she saw Will sitting in the far corner of the carriage. He was wearing his Tommy helmet and clutched a big toy airplane in his hands. He was staring morosely out of the window and it took a few seconds for Brenda to actually recognise him for his face looked drawn and haggard, older somehow.

He looked miserable now, not good company at all. She didn't know if that kind of misery might be contagious. In truth she felt horrible about leaving her parents in a war-torn town and was only being cheerful for the sake of Eddie who was more likely to cry than not if he sensed his big sister was having doubts.

Will had been quite rude to her twice now. The first time after they had sat with Mrs Parsons and he had just run away afterwards, without saying a word. The second time had been at the memorial. Brenda had gone to offer her condolences. She had been very upset still with Jamie's death and couldn't really talk to Mum and Dad about it. She knew it was different for Will, because he and Jamie were best mates, but she had been hoping to share her grief. Instead it seemed Will had not even noticed her, giving only the slightest acknowledgement of her presence.

Then again, he had been nice a lot of the time too. Brenda looked at Margaret Elizabeth's damaged face and supposed all their faces would change one way or another because of the war. She came to a decision.

"Come on Edward," she said as cheerfully as she could.

"Where are we going? Are we there yet?" Eddie asked.

"No silly, we've only just left the station, we're still in Brighton. I just want to sit somewhere else."

"I don't want to," Eddie said stubbornly.

"Well, then you can sit here, while I sit somewhere else," Brenda decided. She started picking up her various pieces of luggage and then carefully lifted up Margaret Elizabeth.

"I think I want to sit somewhere else too," Eddie said quickly and gathered his things, trailing behind her as she walked through to the end of the carriage. He was clutching his blue and white stuffed rabbit which he called Buntings and avoided eye contact with the other children who looked at them as they passed.

"Hullo Will," Brenda said brightly and then, without asking, started depositing her things and sat down. Eddie followed suit, staring at Will with big eyes.

"Oh, hello," Will said dully.

"So where are they sending you?" Brenda tried to peer at his label, but words had been pencilled in hastily and she couldn't decipher them.

"I have to get off at a place called Nickleby," Will said glumly and looked outside again at the last rooftops of Brighton which were passing by.

"Oh," Brenda said. "Eddie and I are to get out at a place called Odesby. I think that's one station further along. Exciting isn't it?"

Will looked at her as if she had gone mad and for a moment Brenda regretted that she had traversed the carriage.

"Spitfire?" Eddie asked longingly.

Will hesitated for a moment.

"Just be real careful with it, alright? It was Jamie's." He said and Eddie nodded eagerly, very gingerly taking hold of the toy as Will handed it over with some reluctance.

"If you break it I shall toss Buntings out of the train window and the foxes will eat him," Brenda said, knowing Eddie well enough to realise he needed an extra incentive. If he broke the toy Will would probably only become even more miserable, especially because it had belonged to Jamie and she didn't know if she could stand that.

Eddie nodded, impressed by the threat and happy to be holding the beautiful toy Spitfire.

"I do hope we will be sent to nice people," Brenda said fervently, expressing her deepest fear in the happiest tone she could muster.

"You mean you don't know?" Will asked with surprise in his voice. It seemed to have brought him out of his shell for a moment and Brenda was pleased.

"Of course not, we will be told at Odesby," Brenda mirrored his surprise. "Do you?"

"My great-uncle. He lives on a farm somewhere north of Nickleby," Will became surly again.

"A farm! How nice," Brenda said.

"I have never met him, nor been at a farm," Will looked out the window again and then briefly flared into frustration. "I am a Brighton boy Brenda; I have no idea what to do on a farm."

"Dig for Victory!" Brenda exclaimed.

"Straight from the plot to the pot!" Will smiled, though a brief shadow flitted over his face.

"I am sure a farm will be terribly exciting," Brenda said wistfully. "Better than a town house. At a farm there is…space."

She meant to say that if the complete strangers she was about to meet were horrible people there might be a place to hide on a farm. A safe place.

Will looked at her thoughtfully and Brenda's fears were mixed with some cheer. She had managed to get him to leave that unhappy isolation he had seemed wrapped in and that gave her some satisfaction. He must be missing Jamie terribly. She already missed Mum and Dad. At least she and Eddie would stay together. Mum had been given the guarantee that they wouldn't be split up and Mum had made Brenda swear, hand on the bible even, that she would take care of Eddie.

Brenda felt pretty grown-up for a nine-year-old when she placed her hand on the Bible and that had made her feel proud.

"Some of those evacuee children from London..." Will said slowly.

Brenda laughed.

"Do you know the Millersons? On West Drive, by Queen's Park?" She asked.

"No," Will answered curiously.

"They had two East End urchins," Brenda giggled. "They came back one afternoon and found that the boys had plucked the parrot and were cooking it in the kitchen."

Will had to laugh at that.

"We had a fancy one in our class," Will grinned. "Wanted to know why we didn't play cricket at school. He used Latin words to try and sound important."

"I remember him," Brenda said. "He wasn't at school long was he?"

"After a week he blew his lid off, because the family he was staying with on Windmill Street showed him how to use the tin bath. The outhouse had already shocked him. He had been..."

Will imitated a mock falsetto posh accent.

"...simply appalled, a totally appalling situation."

Brenda laughed.

"Jamie was better at doing impressions," Will said.

"Jamie was...," Brenda hesitated. "I miss him."

"So do I," Will nodded with a sad smile.

They looked at each other for a moment in mutual understanding, then the conversation moved on to other people they both knew; familiar streets, sweet shops, parks and of course the seafront.

"You know," Will said pensively. "I just hope there are...adventures. I had adventures all the time in Brighton. I don't know if you can have real adventures in the countryside."

"I am sure you can," Brenda answered although she had some doubts. She had a vague notion that Brighton was the centre of civilisation in Sussex. Perhaps the other coastal towns as outposts of that civilisation; she knew them all by name and had even visited some after all, but she wasn't familiar with any towns there might be further inland. She knew Nickleby and Odesby only because she had studied the train's timetable. She had even heard the people in the country spoke funny; slow and laborious. Somehow that fitted her view of countryside life: slow and laborious. "I just hope..."

"The people," Will answered showing that he had been paying attention to her. He became straightforward. "Are you worried?"

"Yes," Brenda admitted.

Will grinned reassuringly.

"If this Odesby of yours is not far from my Nickleby, we should try to meet," he suggested. "We're both Brightonians. We're standing up to the bleedin' Nazis aren't we? We should manage with the country people."

Brenda smiled though she thought he meant it jokingly. The idea of marching through the hinterlands where she didn't know the way was far-fetched of course. She rather doubted there would be an adult who would condone or supervise something like that.

"I don't even know where I am going," she pointed out.

"True," Will nodded. "Try to get word to the Maskall Farm. That's all I know, but maybe somebody will know the name?"

"Maskall Farm," Eddie chirped.

"Yes, send word where you are. I'll come find you two, it'll be my first adventure," Will promised. "Do you want a sweet? I've got lots."

He dug around in his battered suitcase and produced an unbelievably big bag filled with sweets of all sorts.

There followed a learned debate about the best sorts of sweets and all manner of them were tried as the train moved north-east. There was comfort in having someone to talk about to about familiar places and things that were being left behind and a sense that circumstances had cast them in the same boat. For a while, at least, it felt like they were friends.

The train was delayed once as it sheltered in a tunnel after a station master of a small county station had warned them raiders had been spotted in the sky. After that the journey became uneventful; the locomotive chugged industriously, spouting smoke as it pulled the carriages away from Brighton and deeper and deeper into Sussex.

27. WILL

The train rolled to a stop at a station that was little more than a single platform. There was a station master's post the size of a large garden shed which rose above the bare empty grey decking like the superstructure of a submarine. Will tumbled out of the train with all his belongings. He was the only one to get off at the Nickleby train station and began to set his luggage down on the platform. Struck by a thought he rummaged in his bag till he found his pouch of Class-B ammunition and he opened it.

Will turned to see that Brenda had opened the window and both she and Eddie were looking at him with forlorn uncertainty. Will felt the same; the Brighton connection had kept the town alive for just that little bit longer. It was time to say goodbye in many ways now.

"We'll find each other," he promised again.

"We'll try," Brenda said correctively and Will reckoned she didn't really believe in it.

"Maskall Farm," Eddie nodded with full conviction.

"Here," Will pushed the bag which was still half full of sweets in Eddie's hands. "It's for you, don't eat them at all once and share them with your sister."

Eddie nodded solemnly and then broke into a delighted grin as he peered in the bag.

The train driver let his whistle sound and the engine spat out clouds of steam around its great steel wheels further on up the platform.

"This is for you," Will held out his hand to Brenda who tentatively took three round pebbles from it and looked puzzled.

Then her face lit up and she clutched the pebbles tightly. She looked up at Will questioningly as the steam engine hissed into further life and they could hear its pistons start to chug. He nodded, and spoke loud to overcome the engine's hullabaloo. "In between the Halfway Station and Banjo Groyne. I got a bag full."

"A piece of Brighton," Brenda said happily.

"Yes, a bit of Brighton. Take good care of it."

The carriage shook into motion and Will waved goodbye and kept on waving as the train chugga-chood into the distance. When it was gone he looked up to see...

...absolutely nothing.

As far as he could see fields rolled along with the contour of the land. They were interspersed with copses of trees and hedges. He saw no buildings and no roads, just emptiness. It made him feel slightly dizzy and he took a deep breath and turned around fearing the same view. Instead of fields there were trees. A seemingly impenetrable wall of trees which stretched endlessly to his right. When he turned left he saw a similar green wall but one that ended half-a-mile away in a patchwork of fields centred by a small church around which were huddled a score of cottages.

The station master came walking out of his post and came towards Will slowly for he was at least two hundred years old with a bent back and spindly legs. He used a stout walking stick to aid his movement. When he finally reached Will he peered at the boy through the little rectangular glasses that were perched on his beak-like nose.

"How do, chavee?" the station master said in a friendly tone. "Be ye a Sheere-folk 'vacuee from middlin' Lunnon or praper Suth Seaxna from coast?"

"I think so," Will said carefully. He hadn't understood a word the man said except for the word 'coast'.

The station master's fingers reached for Will's evacuee label and lifted it close to his eyes.

"Ah, Mus Maskall, surelye" he nodded. "He aint yetner here now be he chipper? 'T be unaccountable, howsumdever, he'll be anigh I rackon."

Will's head was spinning. Did everyone here speak as incomprehensibly as this station master?

Hesitantly Will pointed at the village to his left, the only visible sign of human habitation in this green expanse that seemed so overwhelmingly devoid of familiarity.

"That be Nickleby," the station master nodded. "Disyer be Nickleby station. Mus Maskall's farm be atween Nickleby and Wolfden, he have ta stride 'cross the Wyrde Woods."

The station master pointed northwards at the mass of woods.

The *Weird Woods*? The name was as odd as the seeming vacuum of life around Will and he sat down on the single platform bench next to the station master's post feeling miserable and utterly alone. If Great-uncle Maskall spoke the same ubble-gubble the station master did then he felt sure his current sense of being deserted might last a long time. He was glad he hadn't just given the whole pouch of pebbles to Brenda; he would need to hold on to something from Brighton. He clutched his Spitfire tightly...something to hold on to from Jamie as well. He missed his mate terribly and tried not to think how much easier it would have all been if they had been evacuated together.

Will felt as if his war was over now. He had let himself be removed from the place where he had sworn to make a stance on the beaches when the Germans attempted to land. Side by side with Jamie and Mr. Hall as they all coolly catapulted pieces of the beach at the Nazis.

"You want our beach? Here it is! Come and get it!" Mr. Hall would have shouted and aimed another pebble at an unfortunate Jerry.

"All clever stuff, no rubbish you Jerry Duckies," Jamie would have imitated Max Miller's brisk cheekiness to perfection.

All three would laugh confidently when the Wehrmacht soldiers ran out of ammo because they themselves had enough ammo to last them a year. You can't beat Brighton. It just wasn't possible. Instead; Will seemed to be nowhere at all, far away from where he belonged at any rate. He might as well have landed on the planet Mongo.

He spotted movement on the road from the village and looked up curiously. It wasn't Great-uncle Maskall yet but a group of young women who looked like a picture of milk maids he had once seen on a luxurious biscuit tin in Parsons Confectionary. He had believed the picture to be historical but those milk maids seemed to have stepped off the biscuit tin lid straight onto the Nickleby road.

Will grinned, he knew exactly what the Halls would do now and since Jamie and his dad weren't around to do it someone ought to. Just to keep the tradition alive. He began to softly sing Max Miller's signature song and as he did so his smile returned. He would find a way to discover an adventure somewhere here in this wilderness. Jamie and Mr. Hall would never be truly gone that far away, he realised and felt less alone because of that thought.

I fell in love with Mary from the Dairy,
But Mary wouldn't fall in love with me;
Down by an old mill stream
We both sat down to dream:
That was when I offered her my strawberries and cream.

We walked and talked together in the moonlight,
She asked me what I knew of farmery,
I said, 'Mary, I'm no fool
You can't milk Barney's Bull.
That's when Mary from the dairy fell for me.

Fate is inexorable. The hands that weave the strands of our possible destinies spin a wide web of connections which can bring together folk who are initially miles if not whole worlds apart. That latter was certainly the case for William Maskall who had arrived right where he was meant to be; on the edge of the Wyrde Woods in which he was to experience many an adventure and in which the war too, would catch up with him again. That story though, will be told in the novel *Will's War in Exile*.

To be continued

Acknowledgements

Many of Will and Brenda's adventures in Brighton during the summer of 1940 are based on recollections by Brightonians I encountered in the most excellent *My Brighton and Hove* living history website, the *BBC's People's War*, and stories related to me by members of the FB pages *Sussex in History, Brighton Past, Marine Square & Kemp Town Brighton Past & Present* and *1940s World*. This also means I have borrowed people's emotions. If it's real funny or touching: That really happened. The same applies to the more dreadful events where the experiences were far from pleasant. I didn't hold back because I hope the reader who didn't experience wartime Brighton will get an impression in what conditions the town's inhabitants gritted their teeth and bravely faced the storm.

For narrative purposes I have taken some liberties with the actual historical sequence of events. Namely bringing the arrival of the Canadians forward by a few months and inventing a fictitious bombing raid before the terrible events on 14 September 1940 (based on later ones) as well as using the St Nicholas Church incident much earlier in the war (with a different plane). Other events, such as the strafing incidents, borrow from a wide range of eye witness reports of such occasions. Alas, I could not discover just when National Margarine was introduced for the cream tea scene. I sincerely hope that no margarine fans will be left disappointed by any inaccuracies.

Any mistakes are mine and I very sincerely hope that I will not cause any offence to anybody, I meant to do Brighton proud for I have come to admire the town's stubborn determination during the summer of 1940 and without Brightonian help this story could not have been written.

For investing their time in one way or another to contribute to *Will' War in Brighton* many thanks to: Bren Hall, Nick Bulters, Kayleih Kempers, the Klomp family, Janna Gürke, Gerrit Orgers, Marcel Vankan, Richard Hornsby, Corin Spinks, Jack Bryer, Liesel Lehrhaupt, Frank Bruggemans, Leon van Assem, Arjen van Assem, Jax Atkins, Lisa Mari Jackson, Carol Whaley, Jeff Beaufoy, Mat Keller, Richard Tree, Lee Sinatra, Joanna Beck, Alan Ogilvie, Mary Funnell, Jacqueline Thomas, Lynda Finnis, James Hewland, Renia Simmonds, Roland Mason, Marie Pullen, Roz Palmer, Peter Beatle, Irene Marriott, Susan Ann Beckett, Mark Oakley, Ashley Leaney, Dan Kimberley, Gill Wales, Philip Knowlton, Barry Somerville, Lis Telcs, Justina Badger Braddock, Sara van Loock, Dave Whatman, Dan Wilson, Carol Homewood, Richard Wright, Mary Taylor, Saskia Gemmell, John Raymond, Kevin Gordon, Graham King, Marion Goodwin, Camilla Markowiak, Louise Yates, Paul Bland and Roland Thomas.

Nils 'Nisse' Visser
May 2015, Amsterdam

CPSIA information can be obtained at www.ICGtesting.com
Printed in the USA
LVOW10s2358240316

480609LV00033B/1301/P